POWDER MONKEY

Powder
Monkey

KAREN SAINSBURY

Weidenfeld & Nicolson

LONDON

First published in Great Britain in 2002

Copyright © 2002 Karen Sainsbury

The right of Karen Sainsbury to be identified as the author
of this work has been asserted by her in accordance
with the Copyright, Designs and Patents Act of 1988.

A CIP catalogue record for this book is available
from the British Library

ISBN 0 297 60765 0

Typeset by SetSystems Ltd, Saffron Walden, Essex

Printed by Clays Ltd, St Ives plc

Weidenfeld and Nicolson
The Orion Publishing Group Ltd
Orion House
5 Upper Saint Martin's Lane
London, WC2H 9EA

With thanks to Richard Francis

For Patrick

CHAPTER ONE

We were crushed together, drifting across the flooded field in the dented metal bathtub. Heavy spring rain had caused the River Frome to crack and shed two feet of greasy water over the stubbled winter barley.

It happened the day after the police arrested Tam for siphoning petrol. He went straight from the police station round to Auntie Fran's house with the taste of fuel stinging his tongue and the stain dribbling down his neck.

He knocked on the door for several minutes. Tired of waiting for an answer, he lifted the steel netting off the pantry window and wriggled through. The smell of rotting meat hit him instantly.

'Six grand each.' Tam stretched out his long legs with satisfaction, pushing Cameron and me to the back of the metal boat, which was now bobbing precariously.

'What did she look like, Tam?' Cameron asked again, although we had heard the story four times already.

It wasn't rotting meat. It was rotting aunt. It took Tam a while to find her as the meter was empty. The house was dark with thick, dirty net curtains. The sun only strained through in the late afternoon. She was lying on the settee with her feet on the suede footstool, and a month-old copy of the *Sun* open on her lap. There was a cup of Bell's whisky on the floor and an economy pint of milk. There was also a bloody enormous spider's web that had been spun over the corpse, from the side of her head to her hip and down to her heel. According to Tam there were at least two thousand flies caught in it. And a moth.

The coroner classified it as death by natural causes. According to the doctor she had suffered a massive diaphragmatic spasm. Auntie Fran had died of a giant hiccup.

'She was covered in these huge blisters, this big. She was all swollen and this green stuff had dried round her mouth and nose. Her skin had burst on her arms and her hair was coming out all over the sofa. Even her fingernails had come off.' Tam was gesticulating wildly, playing to his audience.

I felt a soft wave rise over the side of the tub, soaking my trousers. Tam laughed and with both hands he shook the sides of the tub, sending us all head first into the shit-coloured water.

I felt Tam's hands holding me under the surface. As I opened my mouth in protest, thick water swilled round my teeth. I was heaving and gagging as the water hit my lungs. He held me under for over half a minute. I was light-headed, the blood ringing in my ears. And then suddenly he released me. As I struggled to find my feet and to wipe my stinking hair off my face, Tam was standing knee-deep in slime, his eyes bright and shining as he watched the cars zoom by on the bypass.

'That's what I'm going to buy when I'm eighteen, a big fuck-off car with all the fucking extras.'

Six grand. The three of us were worth six grand each. To be held in trust till we were eighteen. And we were so jealous. Tam was only twelve and he'd seen a dead body. I had to wait till I was eighteen before I saw one.

★

2

It was a while since I had unscrewed the cap on the electric socket and placed my finger inside. On a good day I used to be able to count to twenty before I took it out again, but ten or fifteen seconds was still good. I did it for the current pulsing through my wet finger as I knelt on the concrete step, as someone scored for England in the lounge, and Mam and Da argued on the stairs. It was a precursor to a sex life and just as shocking.

The hillside was illuminated by flames, the air full of burning pieces of hay from Da's barn. The stench of smouldering grass was thick in my lungs. The sheep were in the bottom pen. If Cameron hadn't chased them down the hill they would have stayed and burnt to death, quietly chewing and watching as their greasy wool ignited and turned them into mutton.

Da was beside himself, 'Get the fucking hose from the house. Get the fucking hose.' The hose was already on its way. Tam carefully unwound it from its case and aimed it at the barn. The jet of water hit the flames, but the fire had taken too much of a hold over the three hundred bales. Da had lost the hay and the barn. It was a good time to make myself scarce. There was nothing I could do.

It was six o'clock. Today the Russians had landed a probe on Mars and the world was waiting for the first pictures to be transmitted back to earth. This was a major leap forward in the new space race that had been declared between East and West. We watched it on the black-and-white telly in the kitchen, drinking tea with black hands. The television studio was backed by a large photo of the Milky Way, and curiously the red planet was missing. There was a great close up of Saturn, though. Must be left over from the last space report. Da got

3

up to turn the telly off. It was disconcerting watching a screen that was split by a moving white line.

'It shouldn't have happened. The hay was dry, dry hay shouldn't combust. It shouldn't have gone up like that.' Da licked the soot from his fingers.

This is the start of something, I thought to myself as I watched the scientists point out features of the most advanced probe ever sent into space.

Maria popped round that night. She popped round most nights. We sat on my bed drinking paracetamol and Coke. We chatted for ages, pretending to be high. Later we made ourselves some chips in the kitchen. At nine o'clock Da and Tam came in from the sheep pens. Da looked done in, mud staining the lines in his face.

I didn't wake till ten to ten next morning. I'd fallen asleep in my clothes again. It had been a clear night. It was a bugger having to get up early. Work was a constant drag. If I'd been born ten years earlier I could have queued at the dole office with my mates, popping in once a fortnight for my giro, blowing it at the pub minutes later and then going home to a cooked tea. This couldn't happen any more. Unemployment was virtually non-existent.

Da was in the kitchen, licking stamps and then floating them in his cup of coffee. He looked up as I crashed through the door.

'Not so fucking loud.' Da's eyes were raw from the fire. 'You fucking bugger.' One of the stamps had dropped in the wrong way and was floating belly-up. It was sensible to leave now.

It was a typical early-spring day in Frome. Wet. Wild. Lucky last night had been so good. The sky had been alive with stars. I slipped down Church Row and into Selwood Road, which was still closed as they were taking off the top layer of the old printing works before they turned it into flats: part of a local scheme to lure the eye away from the smoke-stained brick and cracked paintwork. A traveller exploring these parts could easily believe the whole town had been cremated overnight, from the amount of ash that fell on your clothes as you walked through. Mam said it was because people were too tight to have their chimneys swept.

The Griffin on the corner of Austin Street was silent, recovering from another Friday night. The pools of vomit had chilled and the roaches had been brushed away by Mrs Brownlow, who did that sort of thing.

It was half-ten and I was late for work again. I had been working at the Indian takeaway for two months. The owners, the Singhs, were all right, good to work for. The rest of the family had been tragically killed in a plane crash on the way over. Luckily Indira had been wearing a very loose sari and she and her husband had parachuted gently to the ground whilst their nearest and dearest had their heads staved in on concrete. I think that's how the story went, anyway; Indira's English was a bit basic. The job consisted of chopping veg-etables and setting tables, cleaning the large pans they used for cooking, and occasionally retyping the worn menus. The pay was lousy, three hundred rupees a night, but I could eat as much as I wanted, and take home any leftovers from the night before.

Indira was in a jolly mood.

'God, I love Frome. It reminds me of Delhi. It is my home from home,' she sang as she squeezed out her washing and pummelled it on the patio. Sanjit emptied the water from the large plastic tub and refilled it slowly, walking to and from the kitchen with a large saucepan. I watched them from the kitchen window as I scrubbed the potatoes. They were working in silence, their heads were touching as they concentrated on their work. Then I chucked a load of tablecloths in the washing machine and Indira's songs were drowned out.

When I got home I spent the usual half-hour emptying the metal pots of chicken tikka and meat curries into the bin. Monday night leftovers were shit, all chewy meat, probably cat. I scrubbed the smell of garam masala from under my nails and checked the time. Two o'clock: I just had time to get changed and go for a quick walk up to the woods.

The garden was full of empty flowerpots waiting to be filled with the seedlings from the greenhouse. Gardening was Da's thing; Mam hated anything to do with nature. There were twenty or thirty trays of tiny green shoots nestling in the comfort of their heated glass quarters. It was a joke that the greenhouse was actually warmer than our house, which was heated with a small smoky Aga with a tiny ash-tray and the boiler didn't have enough capacity to reach my room at the top of the house, or the bathroom. Mam went mad if we splashed too much in the bath, because the carpet was a bugger to dry. Da fuelled the greenhouse using sheep crap taken down in bin liners from the hillside. That was Cameron's job now that I worked for the Singhs. Da, like many of our neighbours, ran a few sheep, over two hundred after a good spring. He had been raised in a small Scottish village where sheep were the mainstay of life. His flock had been started from two lambs that had been a wedding present to him and Mam from the Scottish side of the family. Prime Scotch lambs that grew and bred well. He only ever grew Scottish breeds. He had started by renting an acre off a neighbour, expanding each year till he had the whole hillside. It was his dream that we would all follow in his footsteps, but farmers were going broke all over, the money was gone from agriculture. Da couldn't afford to pay me. Tam and Cameron had to supplement their income cutting hedges, clearing rabbits, or beating during the shooting season.

It was chilly, winter still hovering at the back of spring. I always think about coats when I'm out of reach of one. I walked as far as the river and paddled in the shallows of the flood and then, with wet trainers, I made my way across the drier fields to the west, past the timber mill, and the coppice woods and out to the main road. The light was fading now. I walked briskly along the edge of the road, causing the odd car to swerve and beep.

The kitchen was damp with condensation when I got home, the top of the Aga covered in steaming saucepans of vegetables for our tea. Mam was leaning against the stove, completely absorbed in a cookery book. The bottom of her blouse was simmering in with the peas. I watched her as I undid my laces. She had fresh lines on her face, steaming in the heat like the veg. I had this nightmare that one day the lines would all join up and her face would disintegrate, and behind the gap three little mice would be winding the cogs to her brain. 'Hello, love.' Mam moved to the left to allow me to tie my trainers to the bar. Her wet blouse flopped out of the water unnoticed. 'Good timing, I'm about to dish up, I thought we'd eat off trays tonight, the footie's on. D'you want to start taking them through?'

Tam and Cameron were on the sofa, their eyes glued to the box, England playing Cameroon in the World Cup. They were enclosed by four walls of peeling pink paper, stained by twenty years of nicotine and the occasional thrown curry. The

7

Hoover was on the floor and a replica football pitch was marked out on the carpet, the boundaries drawn from suction from the nozzle. Mam followed me into the lounge, balancing three trays.

'Get your head out of the way.' Tam took his tea and waved Mam away. I sat on the suede pouffe that Mam had salvaged from Auntie Fran's house. The veg tasted of persil.

'Mam, it tastes funny.'

Da waved his fork in my direction, 'Are you going to let us watch this or not?'

After tea I climbed the two storeys to my bedroom. The view from my tiny sash window was awesome. The River Frome, swollen with the spring rain, was lapping over the banks onto the bordering fields. A large black crow, standing on one leg, was staring at something in the distance, and the brown and white horse who thought he was a stallion kept watch over his imaginary mares. To the east the low hills shone with fresh green new grass, and in the dip a few sheep grazed unconcernedly. These were a Somerset breed, a local favourite for their flavour. Not as succulent as our Scotch ewes, Da always said. I could never tell the difference; I preferred pork anyway. Us MacNabs were only third-generation sheep farmers. Coming from Lanarkshire in the south-west of Scotland, granda had been a lead miner till they closed the mines in Leadhills and he had rented a few acres off the estate and bought himself some lambs from Lanark Market.

It was market day, the town buzzing with people on their way to buy their four big toilet rolls for a pound, and their authentic Indian saris to dress their windows. The three pairs of men's boot socks for two pounds were quite a legend round these parts. I walked past the cul de sac where Auntie Fran had lived. I stopped at the little shop on the corner for a Twix; the man behind the counter, Victor, was deep in conversation with a customer about makes of banana, 'Always buy Fyffe's or any of the South American varieties,' he advised, 'they're the best.' A copy of *Just Seventeen* was open at the counter at the problem page.

When I got home I dug up the cat. He'd been dead for six years, buried under the ivy at the bottom of the garden, surrounded by a small stone circle Tam had chiselled himself. It was Tam who had killed the cat. He had sold its blood to a mate who worked part time at a lab. Tam needed the money. It tided him over after the shooting and before the lambing. Unfortunately the cat needed its blood. Its eyelids went very pale, and it collapsed. I often dug it up, when I was bored or depressed. We had buried him in a bin bag so decomposition was very slow. After six years he still had his fur and his whiskers.

★

Maria closed the door and looked at me expectantly. It was the day after I was eighteen.

'What are you looking for again?'

I could feel the bulge in the pocket of my trousers. Wads of fifty-quid notes, neatly folded and folded again. Tam said you should always sniff notes before you handed them over, because such a high percentage had been used for snorting cocaine. I'd had them all out on my bed that morning, and had sniffed and sniffed with no effect at all.

We were in the scientific equipment shop up Catherine Hill. Auntie Fran's legacy had come through. The shop was full of units and shelves jammed full of glass tubes with rubber siphons and pickling jars in all sizes. A door opened out the back and an old man carrying a tray of Bunsen burners hurried out with his mouth wide open. He was thin and tubular and looked as though if you twisted his head he would burn blue rather than orange. 'Sweet shops next door, missy.' He peered at me long-sightedly and jumped suddenly. 'My God, look at that huge wasp.' He was looking past me, out the door and down the road half a mile. Maria and I instinctively turned and peered. I saw nothing. 'Swizzle lollies, Parma Violets, Blackjacks, they've got the lot next door.' He leant forward and prised my hand off the counter I was resting on. Five finger smears remained.

Half an hour later Maria and I staggered back out into the rain carrying a huge box. The bulge had transferred from my pocket to the hand of the shopkeeper, who carefully sniffed each note before he tilled it.

'You bought an old one?' Mam looked up in surprise. She was reading a copy of *Nursing Weekly* she had slipped inside a *Woman's Realm*. She had been filling out a 'What Is Your Blood Group?' questionnaire when I came in.

'Antique.' We kept our voices low. Da was just outside the back door feeding his tomatoes.

'I thought you wanted an ultra-modern new one?'

'I did, but then I figured it would be really cool to have an old one.'

'An antique one, you mean.' The subject of Auntie Fran's inheritance was a dodgy one. It was a well-known fact that Da had a brief fling with her while Mam was giving birth to Tam, literally. The affair lasted twenty-two hours and it cost Da eight pounds to catch a taxi to the hospital. Auntie Fran had left half of her estate to our side of the family, and half to her side. I have never had any idea whose relation she actually was, if any.

It was the biggest purchase of my life, worth the humiliation of my eighteenth birthday to get it. Mam had insisted on a party. She had sent invitations to all my friends, the sort of invitations you get from Woolworths. She had also sent them out to some relations. But as I had hardly any friends, the old relations made up the majority.

'We'll have games in a minute.' Mam squeezed past a wheelchair with a scarf, a hat and a bar of chocolate.

The sky was incredibly clear. From just x250 I could see Beta Hydra burning at seven times the light of the sun. The planets stood out in sharp focus, hanging in space. This was an excellent position for stargazing: most of the streetlamps had been smashed, so light pollution was minimal.

One night I had climbed up the hillside and seen the Northern Lights. I sat up there till 2 a.m. No one else cared enough to look, except the rabbits and the sheep. We all sat there watching the flashes. A ewe stood on the footpath chewing, transfixed by the sky. I've often wondered if animals chart the night sky, like we do, to keep them off the bogs at the tops of the hills, or to tell them it's time to give birth or to die.

The clip on the lens had broken. I had to hold it in position, but the quality was superb for a piece of equipment that had been made 150 years ago. In the background I could hear Mam moaning to Cameron.

'Next time one of your friends misses the toilet, perhaps you could get them to clear it up. It smells like a sewer in here.'

CHAPTER TWO

There were gypsies brawling outside the Beehive. Six police-men sustained injuries from several hundred wooden pegs that were being hurled across the street. There was a dead dog lying in the gutter, a golden retriever. Its tail was ten foot down the road. I was late again. Sanjit would go mad. I stopped at the Spar for a packet of Refreshers.

Indira was whacking her head against the wall as I let myself in round the back. She was attempting to run off the menus on her new computer.

'Keith, why oh fucking why won't they print straight?'

Maria had come round again last night. Her freckles didn't look as bright as they used to. She had been my only friend at school; we had both been unpopular. The teacher always paired us up for Scottish country dancing. The way she scratched her arm when excited really pissed me off sometimes.

The restaurant smelt of stale poppadams as I struggled through with the Hoover. Cigarette smoke and stale poppa-dams – probably because the entire floor was full of stale poppadams and fag ends. I crunched my way to the far wall and switched the vacuum on. I walked in front of the nozzle, treading on the large crumbs so that they wouldn't block the tube. There was a pile of straw under table 5, probably from the turn-ups of several pairs of jeans. I stuffed it in my pocket for Maria's guinea-pig. There was a pile of dog mess under table 8, which was strange because that table hadn't been taken last night (Tuesdays were never busy). Sanjit sat at the counter with a cup of tea and a copy of the *Sun*. His reading was poor and he didn't like to overtax himself. He glanced up as, with a whoosh, the Hoover bag burst. 'Bang bang.' He smiled at me through a cloud of dust and carried on reading.

There was dinner on the table when I got in. A lamb risotto.

'Hope it's not too chewy. It only died yesterday, so the collagens won't have broken down yet, but I haven't had time to go to Sainsbury's.'

'The rice is nice,' I lied with my mouth full. It was dead chewy.

★

On Sunday we all piled into the Granada and headed south, to Auntie Sage's bungalow in Worthing. It was a painful annual thing. Sage, Mam's sister, lived on the seafront and had a beach hut off-season. 'You can't rely on summer for being hot, so why pay the extra?' We had sat there last November in shorts and balaclavas.

Mam looked out the window in awe as we passed many identical low-slung bungalows, 'Absolutely no character at all. Heaven!'

Da snorted and took his hands off the steering wheel to roll a cigarette. Mam put her hand on the wheel and screamed as an old lady stepped out into the road.

'For Christ's sake, Michael, drive carefully. They walk slower here than back home.'

By the time we pulled up I had bruises on my ribs from the surrounding elbows. We were too big for family outings, and Tam always dug in round corners.

Sage was bailing water from her living room when we pulled up. The house smelt of sewers. 'We're campaigning for a longer outfall pipe. Would you sign the petition while you're here?'

In between buckets we handed round the plastic-covered form.

The seafront was the same as ever. It was low tide and thick clumps of smelly seaweed clung to the pebbles, pebbles that cut your feet when you ran to the water, a trail of blood marking the route back to your towel. Da, Mam, and Sage set up deckchairs and stripped down to their cossies. Sage handed round the Thermos.

It was like we were kids, dredging the rockpools for tiny fish and crabs and then lobbing them at each other.

'It's fucking horrible here.' Tam hurled a crab at a flock of seagulls that were leaving narrow footprints in the sand. With a united squawk they all shot upwards and circled us, crying like malevolent babies. Cameron sat on a breakwater and flicked his lighter on and off, completely absorbed by the flame that was lying flat, away from the wind, almost invisible except for the tiny blue heart. When we walked back up the beach, Da, Mam and Sage were playing Ludo in the beach hut, with the door shut.

There was a man selling fresh fish from a little cart. He was humming 'Greensleeves', stopping occasionally to bang a wriggling cod on the head, like a headteacher gaining attention at assembly.

'Hello, boys. Fresh fish, in a cone with a Flake, only a pound a time.' By his eyes you could tell he was deranged.

Auntie Sage told us later that he had developed a rare psychosis from years of driving an ice-cream van. 'It was the tune, they say, drove him round the twist. People generally use "Popeye the Sailor Man" these days.'

It was midnight when we arrived home. Mam put the kettle on while Da and Tam went up to check the sheep. Mam brought in some kindling and lit the Aga, making a tower of sticks and paper and filling the gaps with little bits of coal.

'Why can't we have central heating like Sage?' She rubbed soap into the black line under her wedding ring. 'Just one flick of a switch and the whole house, instantly warm.' Cameron raised his eyes to the ceiling and I dug my nail into the wooden tabletop.

★

It was still raining in Frome next morning. Dry in every other town in England, fine drizzle in Scotland and Wales, sunny even in the rest of Somerset, just pissing down in Frome.

There was a knock at the door first thing. Outside I found Maria, her hair in rat's tails and her T-shirt soaked through. I noticed that bit first.

'Guess what.' Maria sat on my unmade bed and tucked her feet under the duvet. My room was always cold. 'I've heard from the university. I've got in on the business studies course.'

Downstairs Da was slamming the fridge door, making the herb bottles jump and turn.

'Where's the bloody bacon? Can't a man eat in this house?'

'Oh, right.'

It had been a clear night, until the rainclouds had moved in. I had sat up till three watching Mars, its red glow warming the sky like a fake coal on an electric fire.

15

'How about you? Have you heard yet?'

'I didn't get in.' The letter was squashed into a ball under my bed.

'Oh no.' Her T-shirt was drying in thin lines across her chest. She leant forward to touch my arm. The gesture made me jump. 'Do you want to go out for a drink tonight? We could discuss your other options.'

'I don't really go out evenings. Not when the weather's good, anyway.'

I went downstairs after Maria had gone. Da was sitting at the kitchen table reading the paper. He was looking tired, his eyes a potholer's heaven, sunken in his face. A packet of ibuprofen lay open on the table with contra-indications smoothed flat, as if he had been checking to see if the back pain he suffered from was in fact triggered, not controlled, by the painkillers.

★

The careers office was busy next morning as I crashed through the glass door. The room was full of red-eyed teenagers, plus one man in his fifties who was handing out tissues. Everyone had clutched in their hands a screwed-up piece of paper like the one I had.

'How about catering college? With your experience at the Indian you'd have a very good chance of getting in.' The careers officer looked up from the computer that was choosing a career for me. I chewed at my thumbnail, trying to eat the flap of skin that had been bothering me since yesterday.

'I wanted something more science-based.'

The man sighed and rubbed his hand over his forehead. 'I tapped in science, with all your other details, and all it could come up with was domestic science. There's a course at Bristol with spaces.'

'Could you look up the BSc in astro-microbiology at Bristol, see if there are any places left?'

'You didn't get in. You need A levels. You don't even have science GCSEs. It's time you were more realistic about your options. You could go back and take A levels, but in all honesty they won't equip you with the skills you're going to need in the workplace. And that is your best bet: get yourself a job, or an apprenticeship.'

The computer crashed at that point and I made my excuses.

Da didn't say anything as I put a plate of burnt food in front of him. Every newsagent I had passed on the way home had a headline about Mars on its billboard.

'They say they've found evidence of life on Mars, Da. It's all in the papers, and on the radio.' Da didn't bother too look up, too preoccupied with how to prong a sausage without breaking the fork.

Tam was in the lounge, sticking his tongue down the throat of some girl. It wasn't the same girl he'd been at the pub with last night. She had long black hair that hung down her back like a horse's tail. I switched the telly on, but was unable to turn over as the remote was somewhere under Tam. I tried not to look, but felt my trousers tighten. Tam liked being watched. To him sex was an art and he was up there with Reynolds at the Royal Academy. The girl wasn't so impressed though.

'Get your brother to fuck off, Tam.'

I went into the garden and dug at the wet earth with a shovel. This was the corner Da used for the seed potatoes, which were already sprouting in plastic bags under the sink, and where I had dug a river channel when I was a kid, filled it from a watering can and dammed it to stop the imaginary village flooding.

From the gate at the bottom of the garden you could either go up the hillside, or down the alley, where I used to stand for hours beating the nettles with a stick. There were numerous cracks in the concrete pavement that housed major colonies of tiny black ants that ran so fast they were almost invisible. Sometimes I would capture a load in a Coke can and take them to the imaginary village and remove the dam. The emergency rescue kept me amused for hours.

I knew every inch of the house and garden. Years ago I used to go round with a notebook, measuring walls and corners, documenting the house for posterity. I spent many weeks searching under the downstairs carpets for evidence of an entrance to the Frome Underground, an ancient series of passages under the town that no one knew anything about. This is what happens when you don't have any friends.

Da was still reading the local paper as I went back into the kitchen.

'Got yourself a decent job yet?' He was itching for a fight. To Da a decent job meant getting your hands and boots dirty.

'I've been down the jobcentre,' I lied.

Da looked up and stabbed his finger at the page he was reading, 'It says here they're about to build a new road through the valley. They'll need labourers. It might toughen you up.'

I froze in horror. 'They can't put a new road in. The streetlamps will wreck my field of vision. I'll never be able to see the Northern Lights again either.'

I was rising to it. I knew I shouldn't. Da slammed the flat of his hand against the table, causing me to jump and flinch.

'I lost two lambs this morning. That's what your bloody lights do, they kill my livestock.'

There was no point in arguing.

Upstairs, the door to Tam and Cameron's room was slightly ajar. I mustered all my self control not to look inside, then I looked inside anyway. The room was plastered with pictures of girls pushing their tits at the camera. I was surrounded by four walls of two-dimensional naked women. In the corner was the CD player Tam had bought at Christmas. It was incredible. I didn't dare touch it, in case it had an alarm. Above Tam's bed was an entrance to the loft space. As a special treat, or when I paid him, he would let me have a look around. It wasn't an attic, there were no floors or storage areas, just a series of beams you could wriggle along. We could close the flap behind us and sit in the darkness, the smell of dust and moths overpoweringly familiar and reassuring. The loft space connected to all the other houses in the row, and we used to straddle the beams and ease ourselves along an inch at a time, until the splinters in our bare thighs would bleed and snag on new splinters. There was a fascinating array of pipes and cables, some neatly pinned to the wall, others lying in loops like sheep intestines, and Tam would point out the duodenum and the bowel.

Later in my room I could hear the sound of music coming from the Griffin. Cars kept pulling up outside, and people, laughing and joking, were going inside. I caught sight of Maria with a load of her mates. She saw me, I think, as she turned briefly and looked up, but I hid behind the curtain and when I looked up again she had gone. The Griffin wasn't Da's local, he normally drank at the Bell with the other farmers – but tonight was Tam and Cameron's night: and they were buying the drinks, and Da was not one to miss out on a free pint or two. Where was Mam? Probably at work still. She was always there.

As I looked through my telescope I was aware of a sudden darkness outside. A power cut. I could hear people in the pub screaming, pretending to be scared. This was brilliant because without the streetlamps the sky was free from the normal light pollution. The whole solar system was laid out like a giant join-the-dots picture. I could see the belt of Orion, like church candles at Christmas, the dark broken up by clusters of tiny lights. The lens fell off my telescope at that point, and by the time I had realigned it the cloud was closing in. I lay on the bed for hours, but I couldn't sleep. This terrible feeling of hunger was slowly taking over my body. A thousand exploding pips were popping and bubbling inside my stomach, like a marching alien army heading for my brain. The power was back on now, but I didn't bother with the light as I crept down the stairs towards the kitchen. I nearly screamed as a voice came from the darkness.

'Couldn't you sleep, love?' Mam was sitting in the dark at the kitchen table, a cup of tea in one hand and an empty packet of ibuprofen in front of her.

'I wish people would say something's run out,' she half grumbled. She looked dog-tired. A copy of the *Mail* was open on the table; the headline read: 'More Die as Troops Move in on Helstad'. She caught my gaze. 'It's terrible. They're asking for nurses to go out there. People are dying of non-terminal illness, because they haven't enough staff or medicines to care for them. Minor injuries are turning gangrenous. It's madness.' Mam was a nurse at the Orchard Retirement Home in Culverhill. The Orchard was a big Victorian manor-house with dark corners and cheap margarine. Mam looked at me, waiting for a response. I racked my brain for something sensible to say.

'Shame about that.'

Mam stood up, looking more tired than ever.

'Night, Keith.' She paused by the kitchen door, her dressing gown swishing on the lino, and then she disappeared into the dark hall.

There was a sudden hammering on the front door, and Tam's voice filled the night.

'Let us in, the aliens have invaded. Keith, you're our last hope, let us in.'

Slowly I walked to the front door and fiddled with the latch.

'Come on, Kathy, we've got no keys, let us in.'

There was a strong smell of beer as my two brothers crashed past me. Cameron went up to the toilet, and Tam followed me into the kitchen.

'Should've come down the pub with us; your girlfriend was there.' He slumped down in my seat and picked up the ibuprofen packet. 'Shit, it's fucking empty. I'm working in the morning.'

I couldn't breathe. I sat up with a jolt, the sensation of fabric sticking to my nose somewhat alarming. I looked at my pillow. It was red with blood, soaked through. It was the first nosebleed I had had for six years. Mam used to make me sleep with a bandage round my head to prevent anaemia and to cut down on the washing. I went to the bathroom. Cameron was in there with a pile of *Amateur Photographers* – the magazine, that is, not the genuine enthusiasts.

'Piss off, I am having a shit.' Cameron ignored my banging

and went back to reading about soft-focus lenses or whatever. I looked in the mirror in Mam's room. A face of cracking, congealing, flaking red frowned at me. I sat on the edge of the bed and picked at my skin for a while till I heard the toilet flush.

★

It was past ten o'clock when I heard Da bellowing in the lounge. Mam was stoking the Aga in her dressing gown as I went downstairs, her bare toes curling into a mound of ash from yesterday's fire.

'Fell off the fucking sofa.' Da was rubbing his arm, a bruise already starting to appear on the freckled skin.

'That's why people usually use beds to sleep on.' Mam didn't bother to look up. She wiped her hands on her dressing gown and took some eggs from the fridge.

'Scrambled eggs, anyone?'

I was on time for once as I walked up the road into Badcox and knocked at the takeaway. A strange face appeared round the door and jabbered at me. I shook my head and pointed to my watch. An arm appeared round the door and a finger pointed to the watch that was attached to it. The face started shaking ferociously. We both stood there for a few minutes shaking and pointing until there was the sound of a slap and the face disappeared and was replaced by Indira's.

'Keith, good news, my entire extended family are here. They took the slow boat over. Isn't it marvellous?'

Great, I thought as I walked home again with last week's wages in a little brown envelope. Shame the boat didn't sink.

Maria was coming out of the Spar. 'Hiya. I've got some sandwiches, do you want to come to the park?'

'Yeah, all right. I've got some straw for your guinea-pig at home.'

'Oh, cheers.'

We walked to the park, with our arms just touching. I was aware of how close she was to me, but I didn't like to move away. She chatted cheerfully about her career and her job and her guinea-pig's injured foot while I thought about my own future, without a career or a job. Even the cat was dead. I made a mental note to dig it up again later. It used to like me, used to sleep on my pillow and wake me up in the night to throw a furball on to my pillow. I would get covered in flea bites in the summer. My scratching used to drive Da barmy. 'Someone spray the fucking kid or I swear I'll crack his spine over my knee.'

We sat on the swings and Maria tore in half a pathetic cheese and pickle sandwich that had no butter. There were puddles underneath us as we gently swung back and forth, watching the schoolkids on the playing field opposite scoring for England, their shorts thick with mud. '. . . And in my second year I can choose to specialise if I want, in IT perhaps. Apparently the best students get creamed off by local companies, so I could finish my degree and walk straight into a job.'

'Oh, right.'

Maria could talk for hours, so I let her. The cat would have to wait.

We all went to the Eco's festival that night. We sat in the circle of stones with a bag of candy floss and watched the fire displays. Cameron, who was with one of Tam's exes, looked on in wonder at the flaming bird in flight, and the burning of the wooden horse of Troy. The girl, Marjorie, was bored. She would occasionally flick her tongue into Cameron's ear and then study her nails. At one point I heard her whisper to Maria, 'Tam was never like this. He was a better shag as well,' and she looked wistfully over to Tam, who was with a blonde who worked at Sainsbury's. He was running his hands through her hair and she was breathing deeply, her eyes transfixed by Tam. Maria and Marjorie both watched Tam and his latest conquest. It was like I wasn't there.

The fireworks started with a bang. Cameron and I sat in the amphitheatre whilst the girls went to the toilet. Tam had disappeared, to the pub or back to the blonde's flat or whatever. We got some chips on the way home and sat in the back garden in the dark with the door open and the kitchen light on. Maria and I sat on the concrete step and Cameron stood by the greenhouse smoking a roll-up.

'I wonder if we're going to have a good summer.' Maria looked up at the sky, which was exceptionally clear.

'Are you all right getting home by yourself? I'm a bit tired.' It was too good an opportunity to miss, a bit of stargazing before bedtime.

Maria didn't say much as she threw her chip paper in the bin. 'See you then.' She looked a bit pissed of, I thought, as she let herself out.

I heard Cameron come in much later, heard his heavy feet on the stairs. He flushed the toilet and then his bedroom door closed. There were still people milling about in the street below, a few people wandering in the road, the occasional taxi full of faceless people, who all looked grey in the dark like cats. I couldn't concentrate. In the end I lay on my bed in my

clothes and then it was morning. I got up. I was already
dressed. I went down to breakfast. Then I remembered I
didn't have a job to go to, so I went back to bed again.

Mam was trying on nurses' uniforms in her bedroom. They
were white and creased and too small.

'Keith, if I lie on the floor, could you possibly get the zip
past the half way point?'

On the bed was an old photo of twenty white-clad girls
laughing, frozen in time, their hats suspended in the air. Mam
followed my gaze. 'Best day of my life. I bloody hated that
college.' There was a rip and a gaping piece of flesh bulged.
'Oh damn.' Mam gave up and sat up. She looked horribly
past it.

I went with Mam to The Orchard later. I took round cups of
tea to thirty confused OAPs, many of whom thought I was
their son, even the ones who never had children. One old
biddy grabbed my arm, nearly sending a cup of tea into her
lap.

'You've got to help me. They hit me. They hit me every
day.' I smiled vaguely and walked on. 'A cup of tea, take me
to the toilet, and put me to bed,' another lady rapped at me.
By the smell she didn't actually need the toilet, but I gave her
her tea, and said the nurse would put her to bed in about ten
hour's time. This seemed to pacify her. At half-eleven I was
released from mad people and helped to make up the lunch
trays. There was a machine in the kitchen that could make
twenty slices out of one pre-cut slice of ham. Each piece had
to be handled carefully to avoid it tearing like a cobweb. I
smeared vegetable oil over two whole loaves of bread and

made sandwiches, which I then liquidised. I made a mental note to commit suicide on my thirtieth birthday.

Cameron was washing the car when we got home. He wiped it lovingly with a sponge, hosed it off and then rubbed wax into the paintwork. There were splashes of water on his trousers and soap bubbles on his arms. He didn't say anything as we walked past.

'All right, love?' Mam touched his arm lightly. Cameron raised his eyebrows in response. 'Your father was the same at that age.' Mam unlocked the front door. That surprised me. I always presumed Tam was like Da, not Cameron.

'Whereas, you're more like me. "Stick a kaftan on him and a pair of plaits, and you'd never know the difference," your gran used to say.'

I went for a long walk in the afternoon with Maria, up to Horningsham, through the field with the bull, over the gate and past the pheasant cages, which were full of young birds, flapping and cha-cha-cha-ing. It was quite warm; at last the promise of summer was on the horizon. Maria was quiet, so we walked in silence till we were both sweaty and hot and breathing noisily. I noticed we were breathing in rhythm and our legs had lengthened to the same stride. I became aware of a strong aching, the buzz you get as a kid before you cry. I pulled back sharply. Maria jumped. 'All right? Do you want to sit down for a bit?' Her face was flushed from the exercise, her eyes bright.

'No, we should be getting back.' The light was beginning to fail as we crossed the ford and made our way back to the bypass.

'It's nice we like doing the same things.' Maria slipped her arm through mine. I could smell her sweat. 'There aren't many people you meet that you get on so well with; we're lucky.'

It was pitch black by the time we climbed the hill into Keyford and made our way across town. I dropped Maria off at her front door.

'See you soon?' She looked past me, up the street at a cat who was crossing the road in front of a moving van.

'Yeah, see ya.'

Mam was making a sandwich in the kitchen. She spread a layer of pickle with a knife, put the top piece of bread on, and then wiped the knife on the bread. I shuddered. At primary school, I was the only one who had a smear on the top of their sandwich. I used to sit on my own, or with Maria, with my sandwich upside-down, so that no one would see the ketchup stain.

Mam spoke suddenly. 'I've been accepted on a retraining course. I'm not sure about the start date yet, but it will be soon.'

'Oh, right.' I scratched at a bite on my ankle, the white head flaring quickly to red. It was incredible, the cat had been dead years, but his fleas lived on.

'I don't know if I'll be selected yet, to work abroad, but that's what I want.'

'Oh, right.' The bite was itching like mad. Mam reached into the drawer and fished out a tube of Antisan.

'I just don't know how to tell your da.'

I sat on my bed and stared at the wall above the bookcase. The paper was torn and stained. It hadn't been decorated in years, because Da didn't do that sort of thing and Mam didn't have the time. When we were at school our mam was the only one who worked, except Maria's mum of course, but she was part-time, and it was at the school, so that didn't count. Two or three evenings a week we had to go to a neighbour's house, to wait till Mam finished work, because Da wasn't capable of feeding us. It was such a selfish thing to do.

At eight o'clock we all sat round the kitchen table while Mam dished up. Her face was flushed from frying the fishcakes she had made. I said nothing as she put a plate in front of me. Beads of condensation were running down the kitchen window, the heat from the kitchen smacking on to the cold glass. The blind was usually down by now, but it had been forgotten. Someone had drawn a smiley face on the pane. A long mouth grinned at me as I piled some chips and peas on to my fork.

'I'm thinking about joining that co-operative.' Da was in deep conversation with Tam, who was balancing an empty ketchup bottle upside-down on his plate.

'How's that going to help?' Cameron put his fork down.

'I'll talk to Fraser, see what he reckons.' Tam gave up on the ketchup and used brown sauce instead. Mam took the empty bottle and tipped vinegar inside, put the lid on and shook. 'There's still a bit left.' She knew Tam hated brown sauce.

'I don't see why you can't get to a bloody shop once in a while.' Da resented the interruption.

Mam offered me the bottle and I shook my head. The face at the window was really laughing now, his mouth slowly sliding down the pane.

CHAPTER THREE

The dole office was crowded. At first I thought it was full of people looking for jobs, but then it occurred to me that it was also the location for the Keyford Village fête. People could sign on and then have a go at the tombola. There was a lucky dip by the door, three gos for a pound. I won a can of beans and a packet of wine gums, and I'd just finished when a desk became free in the jobs section. The town was lacking in labour, it appeared. I could work on the roads, or the bins. I could run a big finance company, or help children cross the road. One sad bastard was staring at a blank board, wistfully remembering times gone by.

'Hello, son, can I help you?' I stopped so quickly my own shadow bumped into me. A beard with a suit raised his eyebrows at me. The word 'son' sent an uncanny shiver down my back. 'I'm looking for a job.' It was a stupid thing to say.

'Excellent,' the man beamed out from under his furry mask, 'I shall look upon you as my personal challenge. I'm going to take you, as a raw form, and I'm going to mould you into the government dream. Sorry, am I keeping you up?'

I realised the man was still talking to me and I jumped. The coloured lights and bunting were a big distraction. The overwhelming desire to yawn overcame me. I had been watching a woman try to guess how many beans were in a jar, in a bid to win a fancy doll. I thought it only fair to tell the man of my late night. I didn't want it to look personal.

The beard got up and paid 20p for his go. He guessed three hundred beans, and he must have been right because I saw him at the bus stop later, clutching the doll under his arm. Either that or the stabbed, mutilated body of the woman was lying in a ditch somewhere.

'Now, what sort of job are you looking for?'

'Patrick Moore's.'

'Have you checked the boards?'

I could still hear him as I went down the stairs, past the man on stilts and the face painters and back on to the street with my beans, wine gums, and a bag of candy floss.

'Hello love, what have you been up to? Seen Maria?' Mam looked up from the washing-up.

'No, I haven't seen Maria. Why would I have done?'

Mam smiled but didn't comment. I hate it when people smile knowingly when they don't.

Everyone was looking up at the sky when I went down the road to the corner shop. Breakfast telly had run a feature on the possibility of life in space. A smug presenter with a look to say, 'Everyone's sick of hearing about the war, let's dig up some trash instead,' was sat in front of a giant photograph of the galaxy, which they had transposed somehow, the picture back to front.

Victor was too engrossed in a photo love story to comment on the situation, so I bought a packet of prawn cocktail Walker's and a Coke. I wandered up to the bridge and sat looking over the River Frome, watching the ducks.

'Hi.'

I glanced round as a flash of red made me jump in terror. Maria. She took my crisps and opened them, absent-mindedly picking out the round cardboard prize. She was in a chatty mood, occasionally offering me the crisp bag as she talked animatedly about the big wide world.

'It was great at the Grifffin the other night, you should have been there. Your brothers got your dad completely pissed and he ended up collapsing behind the bar. Tam bought everyone a drink, very flash with his money, not that I like him, because I don't, he's too sure of himself.'

I couldn't help feeling smug about that. The crisp packet hovered my way.

'So, how are you keeping? Got another job yet?' Maria worked in a café in the centre of town. She was into work ethic, was never tempted to take a sickie and walk for hours in the woods.

'No, still looking.'

'I'm doing some work experience at the accountants next week: no money, but what a brilliant opportunity! I'm sick of smelling like last night's chip papers the whole time. Wish me luck.'

She didn't need luck. She had the confidence of Hitler with the dress sense of my dead nan (before she was dead). Maria handed me back my empty crisp packet and then she was gone, darting across the road and into a bus before I could answer.

The news was on when I got in. Mam was standing on a chair in the kitchen, attacking the cobwebs with a brush. 'They are a real bugger this time of year. They get everywhere.' Blue veins were standing out on the back of her leg. I turned the telly up.

'NASA's permanent manned space capsule, which has been orbiting Mars for over a month, has picked up clear heat sources, and scientists are optimistic that they could be generated by living creatures. Speaking from the White House last night, President Bush said that he believes we will soon be making contact with aliens from outer space. Aliens? Bug-eyed space monsters? Little green men? Could it be that at last we will know just how accurate the imagination of people like Speilberg really is? We asked some people on the street what they think.'

Before the news ended there was a quick report about a failed attack on an Albanian weapons store. A primary school had been hit instead, with two hundred children at assembly. 'Don't turn the news off, *Star Trek* is on in a minute.' Mam climbed down from the chair, her hair sticky with cobwebs.

It was ten 'o clock before the sky was pitch black. I stuck the lens to the telescope with Sellotape to hold its position. It was Mars I wanted to see, an image transported thousands of miles from space to my bedroom. I remembered Patrick Moore saying that the first man to set foot on Mars may be alive today. Would he know? Would he spend every night in his bedroom staring up into space, as his wife read to the kids downstairs before nagging him to put that shelf up in the bathroom? And all the time he is watching and waiting until he can make one of the most major steps anyone has ever made. And when he's made that step, would he ever want to come back down from the biggest high of his life? To pop to the chippie on a Friday night, knowing it was all over? I was depressed now, being that man. I shut him out of my head, but I couldn't get rid of that aching sadness in the pit of my stomach, so I went to sleep and dreamt Maria was working in a lingerie shop. When I woke the ache was even worse. I looked out of the window. It was still dark.

I wasn't sure why I had woken, until I heard Mam calling up the stairs, 'Keith, that was your da. He wants you up at the barn. Some kids on bikes have been bothering the sheep. Half a dozen or so have started lambing.'

It was still a clear night. 'Oh, Mam, can't Tam or Cameron go? I'm busy.' I opened the door and yelled down the stairs. 'They're over at the pub. They won't be in any state to stand let alone deliver. I'll get you a Thermos for Da. Can you grab a torch on your way?'

The world was full of baaing as I climbed over the wall at the bottom of the garden, crossed the little lane and took the footpath through the copse and out on to the hillside. This was Top Hill, where Da rented his grazing. It was notorious locally for UFO sightings and magnetic fields and anything like that, and no one else would take it because of the high number of animal mortalities. But it wasn't eerie. It was exhilarating being there that time of night, close to nature. There was the sound of screaming as an owl took the ground from beneath a baby rabbit. I could hear the sound of sheep as I climbed, the harsh frantic bleating of an animal panicking. I could make out some fencing ahead and I headed for it, thankful for the moon.

'Keith, that you?' Da made me jump.

'Look at the moon, Da, it's completely full.' It was a stupid thing to say, the sort of thing you say when you are nervous.

'Never mind the fucking moon. Here.' He flung a wet bundle at me. He despises me, I concluded. He wants Tam or Cameron, but he's got me. I picked the lamb up and massaged it, offering it to its mother. With a shake of its head it sniffed for the source of milk it could smell and started struggling for its feet. I let it go.

'Keith, here, stop fannying about.' Da was holding a distressed ewe who was all but done in. I took her head and shone the torch at her rear end. The owl flew overhead, hooting loudly. He landed on a branch, probably waiting for afterbirths. He was confident in the dim light, the baby rabbit turning to pellets inside his stomach. The ewe stumbled forward on to her knees. 'Hold her steady, will you? Keep your eyes on what you're doing.'

Before I knew what was happening the ewe was down, her breath rasping in her throat. A dead lamb was half protruding from her back end.

'She's had it.' Da was already moving on to the next sheep.

'She's still breathing, Da.' My voice must have sounded hysterical. Da didn't answer. And then I realised that it was my breathing I could hear. I disentangled myself from the dead sheep and followed him.

It was close to 3 a.m. when we finished. We walked back to the house together. Mam was sitting at the kitchen table reading a novel.

'Look at the state of the pair of you. Are you finished?'

Da took off his hat and scratched his forehead, leaving a mark. 'We've come in for the night.'

'I'll put the kettle on.'

No matter what time of day or night it was, a cup of tea was the answer to everything. Mam took a packet of tea bags from the cupboard; I took my boots off and went upstairs. As I washed in cold water in the bathroom, I could hear Mam and Da talking in whispers.

'Got most up, despite Keith.'

I fell asleep thinking about the dead sheep.

★

I went down the jobcentre early next morning. The town was
quiet first thing. I called in at the corner shop, where a strange
woman was serving behind the counter. She was fiftyish and
was reading a copy of *Rustler* inside an *Automobile Weekly*.
Must be Victor's wife. The phone rang as she was serving me.
It sounded as if it was from the hospital.

'OK love, I'll bring some clean things in with me. See you
later, take care, bye, love.' Must be his heart. I knew reading
all those copies of *Just Seventeen* would be bad for him.

There was an air of excitement round the boards today. Da
was right: they were looking for labourers for the new road.
The place was full of people pushing and shoving like OAPs at
a jumble sale. A woman in her sixties kept swatting the ankles
of the people in front of her, then gesturing sideways that it
was somebody else. The atmosphere was menacing. Perhaps I
should come back later. As I left, three security guards, who
had been taken on especially, stepped in to calm things down.

'Hi!'

I jumped as a box of tea bags spoke to me. I was in the
Spar, picking up a chunky-veg pizza for tea. Maria's freckled
face smiled at me through a shelf and I was reminded of a film
I'd seen once.

'Don't do that.' I swept my shattered nerves into a dustpan.

'I've got a new job, as a filing clerk at Tilbury's, the building
merchants. They're being really good about my work experience. They say we can work round it.'

'Oh, right, good for you.' I tried to look excited about
filing.

'Well, what do you think?'

'It could be the start of something big.' Yes, that sounded genuine.

'What? No, not the job. What's different about me?' She had a large spot on her chin, a thin white worm pushing through the head of it. 'I've had my hair bobbed, I thought it would make me look older, more stylish. I'm not sure, though, what do you think?'

Come to think of it, it did look better, less Bristol Zoo, more filing clerk, somehow.

'It'll keep it out your eyes. You can always grow it out if you go off it.'

I called back into the dole office later. Things had calmed down. Two of the security guards were outside with rolled-up sleeves, smoking cigarettes. Inside, a clerk was sweeping up a load of bus tickets and benefit books that had been dropped in the excitement. There were claw marks on the boards, the job cards shredded. Round the room was bunting left over from the fête. There was only one desk open, manned by a woman with a flannel over her eyes. Everyone else had been sent home. When I left I had five full-time jobs, all of which were due to start tomorrow. That's it, I said to myself, as I walked out of the building. The end of my life starts here. I stopped at the park on the way home and went round and round on the roundabout. When I checked my pockets later, the cards had vanished. My money was still there, and my keys; just the names and addresses of all those jobs, completely vanished. Fate.

★

It was Maria's birthday on Thursday. She was having a disco in the Civic Hall to celebrate the joyous occasion of her eighteenth. After great deliberation I bought her a packet of pens and some Tipp-Ex. The Civic Hall was a large room with a stage up one end, fronted with long curtains that didn't close properly; I remembered that from Mam's amateur dramatics days. Maria was wearing a tiny dress made of blue sequins. Bit cold for this time of year, I would have thought; I was still wearing a jumper.

There were thirty or so people present. I recognised Maria's parents in the corner and waved but they didn't see me. They were moving in rhythm to a cover of an Abba song, though when it finished they kept going. It was too early for a party. It was still light outside, the disco lasers hardly showing. It was cheaper to hire the hall between 7 and 9 p.m., and they didn't have a drinks licence, which was a shame, I thought, as I glugged back my orange juice.

Maria touched my arm. 'Are you having a good time?'

At that point I was standing in the corner looking at the pictures the Scouts had pinned to the wall.

'Yeah, great.'

Maria didn't look convinced. 'Have you had anything to eat? There's crisps and things.'

I shook my head.

'Will you come out with me tomorrow night, just the two of us?' She was looking at me intently. I found it difficult to look back at her, straight.

'Yeah, OK.'

'Meet me at the Griffin at eight.'

She was gone before I could answer. I racked my brains to remember what the forecast was.

*

I was up bright and early next morning. The effect of too much to drink was that I peed neat orange juice down the toilet. The kitchen was empty when I went downstairs. I walked down the road for a paper. The town was busy, the pensioners out in force, pension day. I sat on the wooden bench with my feet sticking out on to the pavement, opened a packet of cigarettes and lit one. No one commented about my feet or looked disapprovingly at my fag. I was too old to shock. Life was so fucking boring. Within ten minutes my legs were itching for a walk. I was getting quite fit, the muscles scraping together to cover the bones in my legs. I was restless so I ran up and down the steps by the bridge for ten minutes till the itch stopped and then I had another fag. Thank God I wasn't stuck in some nine-to-five job, I told myself as I walked home again. Just imagine how bored I'd be then.

The forecast had been bad for that night: heavy rain and low cloud, but at ten to eight it was as clear as a bell. Fuck. I looked over to the Griffin. It was still early, but people were starting to mill about. Had I made a definite arrangement with Maria? She was probably meeting some girlfriends as well. I got out my notes and found my place from yesterday. I went downstairs and made four rounds of cheese and banana sandwiches and found a bottle of Coke in the pantry. Tam and Cameron were chatting merrily as they got ready for their big night out. The smell of aftershave reminded me of toilet cleaner: must be some cheap stuff from the market, doubles as fly spray.

I climbed the two flights of stairs back to my bedroom and settled in. It was nearly half-past eight and the sky was streaking with darkness now. I only had about an hour and a half to wait till blackout. I glanced down at the Griffin and shot back guiltily behind the curtain. Maria was standing outside the pub, looking up. She was wearing a black dress and high heels. She must be meeting others, couldn't be waiting for me. I peered out again at five to nine. She was still there, looking at her watch. I felt bad. I looked at my cheese and banana sandwiches, but didn't feel hungry. The sound of voices made me peep again at ten-past. Tam and Cameron were talking to Maria, both shaking their heads: probably putting the boot in. Maria looked uncertain what to do, and started to walk home, but Tam stopped her and they all went into the pub together, with Tam's arm round Maria's waist. Bloody typical. Why couldn't they leave well alone? It was a clear night, but I couldn't concentrate, looking out the window every ten minutes. Tam better not be making a move: he could look convincing, but he was only ever after one thing.

I tried to stay awake, but the last few nights were catching up on me. When I woke up next morning my face was in a plate of uneaten sandwiches.

★

It was yet another morning with no job, no money and no prospects. Mam was gutting a newborn lamb on the kitchen table. Tam sidled in with big black shadows swinging from his eyelids.

'Has the paper come? I want to check the results.'

Mam moved the carcass to check the date of the paper it was lying on.

'Oh sorry, love, it has.'

'That's my bloody *News of The World*, and you're gutting a lamb on it!'

Mam's forehead was furrowed with concentration as she picked up a sharp knife and made a fresh incision. Tam slammed his fist on the table with annoyance, causing the lamb to bounce.

'Hey, careful. I'm not gutting it. I'm giving it a post-mortem.'

Tam shook his head. 'You're round the twist — waste of good meat.'

I squeezed past Tam to get to the fridge. He stuck out his foot and I hit the fridge head-on.

'Keith, be careful.' Mam looked up disapprovingly. 'Anyway, it's not a waste. We can still eat it. This makes far more sense to me than reading a textbook. I miss all that hands-on stuff. Your sandwiches are in the breadbin. Take Cameron's for him, will you?'

Tam took the carrier from the breadbin and left, slamming the door, but not before he had given Mam a dark look he had inherited from Da. Da's side of the family were all like that. Granda MacNab had hated women since his wife had walked out on him when Da was just a baby. She had come back a year later to deposit another baby on him — Uncle Geoff — and had gone again. Left with bringing up two boys, one of which wasn't even his own, his love of women wasn't too great. He wisely moved house as well, with no forwarding address. Mam's eyes were shining as she hooked a piece of hair behind her ear, leaving a blob of blood on her cheek.

'Look at this, Keith, I've made an incision here and here so that I can . . .'

There was a knock at the door. It was the postman, who incidentally was Victor's brother, Arthur. He had round red cheeks and was puffing from carrying his bag. Give him a red and white jacket and he'd be a dead ringer for Father Christmas. He handed me a sheaf of letters and a package, addressed to me. As I closed the door Mam shouted out, 'Did

40

you ask after Victor?' But I left her to her operation and pounded up the stairs to my bedroom. I looked at the package. This was a big secret. This was the thing that was going to save me from a lifetime of unskilled jobs, or whatever the career's adviser had said. I tore open the envelope and a letter with BRISTOL UNIVERSITY stamped across the top dropped out.

Dear Mr MacNab,
Thank you for your interest in Bristol University. I am afraid that you need first to apply through UCAS. A place on next year's course would be dependent upon your A level results, which for this course would need to be ABB.
Admissions.

I couldn't believe it. I flicked through the first two chapters of my book, *Observations of the Red Moon*, which I had sent to support my application. I looked for fingerprints, coffee stains, any evidence of any interest in the information that had taken me five years to collate. All there was was the brown curry smudge on page 60, and the page the printer had run off a bit wonky. They hadn't even fucking read it. What hope would I have taking A levels, when my science GCSE had been so crap? What a waste of time. I didn't even let myself think of that smug git, the career's adviser. The more I looked at the letter the more I was convinced that Professor Hartley, the course director, probably hadn't even seen my work. The bureaucrats at the front desk wouldn't want to worry him with any old rubbish that they had been sent. The only way forward was to get my work directly in Hartley's hands, and then, come October, I would be on the course that I was born for, a BSc (Hons) in astro-microbiology. I could send it to his home address, that was the next move. I looked through my file and found the letter I had from him when I wrote, via the telly, to ask what make of telescope I should buy, two or three years ago now. He had replied three months later on good-quality headed paper that he doesn't reply to fan mail normally, but to contact a local supplier. The letter was signed by Hartley, though I didn't think his initials were PP. I stuck a label over the envelope my manuscript had been returned in and resealed it with Sellotape. I'd post it on my way into town.

CHAPTER FOUR

The street was full of broken glass from a small window in the Griffin. The landlord was out in his pyjamas, taping a big piece of cardboard over the hole with silage tape. It was Sunday morning and Frome was a ghost town. Even the corner shop was closed. I wandered round an empty Woolworths and bought a giant bar of chocolate. The girl on the till opened her scarlet eyes long enough to recognise me.

'Good night at the Griffin last night, should have been there,' she croaked, her mouth raw from cigarette smoke. She was a friend of Maria's, a real hardcore party goer. There's not many who could survive a night at the Griffin and get up to work at Woolworths the next day.

'I work nights.'

'Really? What do you do?' She seemed faintly interested. I rested my arm on the counter.

'I'm writing a book.'

Her eyes closed. 'They're looking for labourers for the new road; my brother's applied.'

'I'm going to university.'

She opened her eyes and spat out a laugh. 'Ow, that hurt.' She clutched at her chest, 'University! You, Keith? Thought you failed your GCSEs?'

There was a large display stand nearly blocking the way out. How naff. It was an alien stand – posters, keyrings, mugs, diaries, everything depicting the same near-human face, with the big, black, pupil-free eyes. How typical that someone would try to cash in. They always do.

I climbed to the top of Da's hillside and looked out over the valley. There was a disturbed patch of earth where Da had buried the sheep carcass. Below me I could see three or four JCBs moving across the valley floor, slowly ripping up the turf and exposing bare earth. It was good soil down there, peaty black and full of worms. It had started, then. Two rows of markers stretched for as far as I could see. A huge sign had been erected to the left: WHATTELL AND LIPLEY CONSTRUCTION LIMITED. The construction may be limited, but the destruction wouldn't be. There was a big rock that Da liked to sit on mid-morning, right at the top of the hill, so he could gaze over his territory. You could just make out the chimney on our house, through the trees. The rock was covered in lichen and was almost impossible to shift. When I did finally manage to move it, a deep imprint was left in the ground, surrounded by fag ends and the elastic bands used to de-tail the lambs. I rolled it to the edge of the hillside and let it fall. I had visions of it gathering speed and smashing the large white sign below, but it stopped just out of reach and settled into the grass.

Mam was in her bedroom when I got back. She and Da had had separate rooms for years, which is why Tam and Cameron shared theirs. She was sorting through a pile of clothes, looking even older than normal. She looked up to find me skulking in the doorway. 'Oh hello, Keith. You couldn't chuck that pile in the bin bag, could you?'

She had met Da when she was nineteen, just finishing nursing college and looking for her first job. She had been brought up in London, where her side of the family, the Bowlers, still live. She had come to Frome for a week's holiday between interviews at Guy's and Bart's. She never went back. She was pregnant, married and trapped within three months.

'I've got a date, to start the course.'

It took me a moment to think what she was talking about.

'You're going then – where?'

'Ultimately to Albania, to Helstad, but initially the course is in Bath. I'll be going twice a week for training. It's going to be a hell of a culture shock.'

'Does Da know yet?'

'No, and he mustn't. I'm relying on you not to tell him.'

'Not much chance of that. We don't talk.' I picked at a scab on my leg.

'That's the other thing. Just because things didn't work out between Da and me, it musn't affect your relationship with him. I want you to try, to really try.'

'Just because things didn't work out between Da and me.' It suddenly hit me that it wasn't just a job she was accepting, it was a new life. She was abandoning us. She'd given up, and was looking for a way out. When had things got that bad? I suppose I couldn't pinpoint it because it had always been bad. She must have read my mind, been expecting a reaction, because she sat down next to me on the floor.

'I'm not deserting you. You're eighteen years old. I had planned to wait until you'd all left home, but there's no sign of that. I need my life back. It's been too long. I don't expect you to like it, but try to understand.'

How could I? We were her life. She shouldn't need more than that.

There were gypsies parked on the verge next to the field with the skewbald horse in. They had brought five skinny ponies with them in a big lorry and spent every evening trotting them at high speed up and down the road in traps. Every night you could hear them laughing and arguing into the small hours, sitting around a large bonfire that gave off too much light. The landowner had tried to fence the verge to keep them out the year before, but they had ripped the posts out and burnt them with great merriment. They came for a few weeks each year and went again. The horse was excited. Now he had some real mares to protect as well as the ones in his head. He kept a vigilant watch on all the proceedings.

We camped in the woods behind the house that night. Tam had the tiny tent he had bought from the shop down Cheap Street. Cameron and I had Da's old Scout tent, a huge un-waterproofed brown canvas thing without a groundsheet. We put our sleeping bags straight on the earth. There was a strong smell of sheep shit inside the tent. It was great to be out though, sleeping rough and all that. Tam lit the little gas stove that had been on special offer with the tent. He never did things by half. I opened a can of spaghetti hoops and cooked them over a low heat.

'We need a fire.' Tam was obviously feeling the cold. 'Get some wood then, Kathy.'

Cameron and I spent half an hour dragging big branches and snapping twigs to make kindling. It was the wrong time of year for camping. The kindling was green and wet, so was the ground. Dark clouds were edging across the sky, slowly creeping up on us. Mam and Da had been arguing in the kitchen when we made our way out of the back gate and up the hill, Mam's arms crossed against her chest, Da's finger aiming like a dart at a board. (When the cat was alive he used to jump on to the worktop and up to the top of the cupboard to avoid a kick up the arse.)

Da retreated as a wooden spoon came into contact with his balding head. We were best out of it.

Cameron struck a match and with a lot of blowing the fire smoked into life, small orange flames coaxing each other round the logs, sparking on the bark, and then hissing at the sap that dripped from above. The air was full of the smell of burning pine, a primeval smell that made your heart pound.

'This is all right, innit?' Tam called from behind the flap of his tent. He had disappeared early after supper with several cans of lager, a porn mag and a little portable telly he had bought from Argos.

'Yeah, great,' Cameron and I agreed as the first spot of rain fell on my head. Within seconds it was pissing down. The fire spluttered for a bit, then gave up. We retreated into our tent, but there was no escape from the torrent that poured straight through the canvas, which was as effective as a sieve. We lay in our soaking sleeping bags and watched puddles turn the floor to mud. It took me ages to get to sleep, but I must have done at some point because when I woke the sky was clear, a weak sun steaming the wet trees. I knew this the instant I woke, because the tent had gone.

'There must have been another bag of pegs somewhere.' Cameron sat up and rubbed a splash of mud off his cheek. From Tam's tent we could hear the sound of an electric razor. Cameron's mobile rang at that point.

'Hi, love, breakfast is ready.' Mam's voice was unmistakable.

We found our tent as we walked back down the hill,

hanging in a tree. By all the crap under it, half of Da's sheep had used it as a shelter overnight.

There was a rave that night at a farm just out of Frome, on the Maiden Bradley road. Twenty quid a ticket saw the farmer with more profit than the sheep he'd sold at market. Da was furious that one of his fellow-toilers had sold out, but Tam and Cameron were going anyway.

At five to eight there was a knock at the door. I was in my pyjamas, ready for an early night after so many late ones.

'Hello.' Maria's new smooth head was silhouetted by a streetlamp. 'Have I got you out of bed?'

I wasn't sure if I should mention the other night or not. I thought not.

'No, I was just going to have some cornflakes.'

She wasn't mad with me. That made me feel worse.

'Well, you can't. You've got to get dressed. We're going out.' She flashed two tickets in front of me. Without reading them I knew what they were for.

'I dunno, Maria.'

'They cost me twenty quid each. I won't have you say no.'

She sat in the kitchen with Tam while I got ready. There was a lot of giggling coming from there, which got on my nerves. When I came down Maria was drinking a beer with Tam sitting too close. They were deep in conversation. They didn't notice me at all.

'Shall we go then?'

They both jumped and got up, Maria more quickly than Tam. We all trolled out into the night and it annoyed me that Tam managed to open both the house door and the car door for Maria. He was so fucking smooth.

'Nice car, Tam.' Maria ran her hand over the upholstery. I

thought she hated cars. She'd looked very upset when I'd told her about the new road cutting through the valley. 'It's all right, innit?' The car was Tam and Cameron's pride and joy. They had Auntie Fran's inheritance to thank for it. They had spent a lot of money on it, though a car was a car as far as I was concerned. Maria was too easily impressed.

'Wow, it's got electric windows, and a CD player.' For some reason she was in the front with Tam, and I was in the back with Cameron. Well, the reason was Tam had engineered it that way. Maria looked through the CDs in rapture and chose a Fossil Monkeys album. We drove along to the lyrics of 'What About the Dog?'

The sky was still streaked with light to the east. It would have been a very good night for astronomy. There was a lot of chatter coming from the front of the car, and complete silence in the back. Cameron seemed as put out as I was. The entrance to the field was thick with mud rutted by tractor tracks. By the time we had showed our tickets and caught up with the small crowd that was amassing, we were also thick with mud half-way up our legs. As Maria was wearing a short skirt, she wasn't that impressed. The crowd was gathered round a tiny stage made of straw bales topped with boards. A runner was plugging wires into the generator behind. Tam and Cameron seemed to know a lot of people and Maria and I were suddenly alone. Well, as alone as you can be in a field full of people.

'Do you want a drink?'

We each bought a pint of warm beer in a flimsy plastic glass that made you dribble. It was imperative to wipe your mouth after each sip to avoid spraying. Maria was animated, her straightened hair frizzing in the damp. She squeezed my hand.

'Thanks for coming.'

One tiny fleck of rain landed on my face. 'Won't come to much.' I studied the cloud.

Maria looked impressed. 'You're so clever, knowing about the weather.'

Within half an hour we were soaked through. I don't remember ever experiencing such heavy rain. Maria was shivering, and I would have offered her my jumper, except I was cold as well. No point us both getting pneumonia.

Suddenly there was a flash and the tiny stage burst into light. Some obscure local band trudged across the slippery boards in Hunter wellingtons and Barbours. 'One, two, three, four.'

We couldn't hear the rain after that. Any lack of quality in the music was made up for in volume, and even I began to relax. The drink was going to my head and it was going to be a good night after all, I could tell. Tam and Cameron appeared behind us and we mouthed conversation. My ears were throbbing, I'd never heard anything so loud. Tam bought us more drinks. The band were sounding quite good now, and the atmosphere was buzzing. Tam disappeared again and came back with hot dogs. I hadn't realised how hungry I was. Tam's eyes looked very bright and dark, and he was unusually chatty. Cameron was drawing on a joint, holding, then exhaling with satisfaction. Maria took a drag and offered it to me, but I shook my head: I felt unsteady enough. The band finished and another came on. Tam vanished again and came back with a burger from the van. I could have eaten a horse, I was so hungry. Tam was watching me as I ate, with a malevolent smile that I couldn't figure out. The rain had stopped now, but no one else noticed. I was desperate for a piss after my two pints, but I didn't like to say so to Maria. She was enjoying herself, despite the fact that her rebellious hair had frizzed terribly with the rain and her mascara was running down her face.

I was beginning to feel a bit ill. Must be the drink. My legs weren't doing what they were supposed to and my eyes wouldn't focus. I kept having to rub them to prevent everything from distorting. Maria startled me by leaning forward and giving me a kiss on the cheek. She murmured something which I didn't catch, because as she pulled away her face distorted into the devil's. I rubbed my eyes and looked again: still the laughing mouth and horns. Maria's voice sounded distant and robotic. I felt I was doing something wrong but I couldn't work out what it was. The music was changing too, I noticed, as if the batteries were running low, but there weren't any batteries. What was wrong with me? I caught another devil looking at me, who could have been Tam. He opened his mouth and laughed and I could see the lining of his stomach. Maria's voice again, nearer this time, difficult to make out, as if she was swimming underwater.

'What's he on, Tam? What have you given him?' I remember thinking of foetuses inside wombs, as my legs rolled over my head and I was spinning suspended in the air. Then it all went black.

The accident and emergency ward was full of drunks and junkies. I was just another one in on a Saturday night, covered in mud and smelling of urine. The nurse looked very grim as she checked my blood pressure. I slumped in my chair, watching pink and purple bubbles burst in front of my eyes. Mam was sitting next to me. I could feel her anger through the plastic chair. A doctor came to give me a lecture, flapping his wings in annoyance as I didn't register.

'When will he come down?' Mam bit at her nails.

'Could be another ten hours or so, and then he'll have flashbacks for the rest of his life.' The doctor was already moving on to the next patient. 'Just how silly will you feel when you're seventy, Keith?' Providing I haven't already been hit by a bus or developed cancer, I thought vaguely as I floated gently round the foyer.

Mam drove home faster than usual because she was so angry.

'Wait till your father gets home,' she hissed, slamming her foot on the brake as a cat ran out in front of us. Da had in fact gone to bed and we could hear him snoring as we stepped into the chilly hall.

'Bloody Aga must be low. Couldn't someone have put some bloody coal on?' I had never seen Mam so het up. 'Oh, just go to bed.' She disappeared outside with the coal scuttle. I did. Eventually. When I'd found the room.

★

The sun was menacingly bright when I woke next morning. There was a tapping at the door and Maria stuck her head round.

'Sorry, did I wake you? I came to see how you are. I've brought you some grapes.' I was very conscious of the fact that I was still in yesterday's clothes. There was a nasty smell that I didn't want to have to explain, and I still had my muddy boots on. God, no wonder my bloody legs ached.

'Hi.'

It was past six when I'd finally gone off to sleep, when the mad colours had shrunk to dots and the buzzing in my ears had subsided, and the adrenalin pumping round my body, which felt deliciously nice, had ebbed.

'Shit, you look pale. I told Tam what I think of him. It was a mean thing to do.'

'What?' I had no idea what she was talking about. My hands were shaking, I noticed, as they rested on the duvet.

'Tam put a tab in your burger. Didn't you know?'

And I thought it had been the alcohol. Oh shit.

'I'll see you later, OK? I'll let you sleep now. It was great last night though, before – you know. Anyway, bye.'

I listened to the sound of her feet going down the stairs and closed my eyes. Wait till I saw Tam. 'Wait till your father get's home.' Oh shit.

I got up and went to the bathroom, where I stripped off my mucky clothes and had a long hot bath. I managed to clog up the drain with mud and spent an extra half an hour with a piece of wire down the plughole. I could hear the sound of arguing coming from downstairs. Mam's high-pitched, hysterical voice: 'It's a cry for help, Michael. We can't ignore it.'

'It's a stage he's going through. The others did it.' Da wasn't angry or concerned. I wasn't sure how I felt about his reaction.

'It's more than that. This isn't like him. I'm worried.'

'Stop fussing. When are we having that lamb I brought home?'

He didn't care, it struck me as I listened. Mam was trying to spark a reaction that wasn't there, wasn't capable of being sparked. That hurt.

CHAPTER FIVE

Arthur didn't look impressed as he handed me a parcel on Monday morning.

'I've carried that bloody thing up every effing street in bloody Frome. If I'm not in hospital with bloody Victor tomorrow it will be a fucking miracle.' It was addressed to me, and I took it upstairs to open.

> Dear Keith,
> Thank you, thank you, thank you for sending me your wonderful work. You are a genius and soon the whole world will know it. I don't want you *on* my course, I want you to teach it. I am humbled to know you.
> Yours respectfully,
> Paul Hartley

Well, that's how it should have read, if there had been a letter. My manuscript was there, and a compliments slip, but nothing else. What was that supposed to mean? I waited till I heard the front door bang before I went downstairs. Mam was on the phone in the kitchen.

'I'll see you Tuesday, then. Well, I am a bit nervous really, I know. OK. Bye.'

I poured myself a cup of tea from the pot on the table.

'That was Wendy from the relief organisation, about my first training session.' Mam picked up a dishcloth and wiped the drips I'd made.

'You're definitely going, then?'

'I don't know. What with your stunt last night, I don't know what to do. Is that why you did it?'

There was no point getting into this one. I went into the lounge and turned the telly on. The topic of conversation was Mars yet again. There were some stunning pictures of Mars on the Beeb, and on ITV a couple were being interviewed about their alien abduction.

'They experimented on me, brainwashed me and yet they were so gentle. There were all these flashing lights and a huge on-off button.'

I had to get on that course. When Mam flew to Albania, I wasn't staying here, with them. That was the only fucking thing I was sure of.

I waited till Mam began hoovering upstairs, and phoned for a taxi. I didn't have any money, but the housekeeping tin had forty quid in that I could pay back later. I walked to the end of the road and sat on the kerb and waited. After ten minutes a cab pulled up.

'Towfield Court, Bristol, please.' I had, clutched in my hand, the letterhead sent to me all those years ago.

The taximan was a manic depressive, screeching out with laughter one minute, and the next sobbing into his sleeve. I made a mental note to go by train next time, as we veered on and off the pavement, the driver beeping the horn and shouting, 'Maniac' at leaves on the road.

I didn't know Bristol at all, and neither did the taximan, so we crawled round for two hours with me directing him from a map. At last we entered a leafy suburb, full of large Georgian town houses set back behind trees. Towfield Court sounded like a council estate, but it definitely wasn't one.

'Stop the car. It's this one.' The taximan sobbed with relief and then made me jump by a sudden peal of laughter. 'Wait for me.' My heart was on a pogo stick as I crunched up the gravel to the front door. Under my arm was my manuscript, a bit tattered round the edges now, but I hadn't dared run off a new copy for fear of the cartridge running out. The big bay windows in front of me were obscured by curtains and the whole place looked deserted. I knocked on the door. No answer. I waited for five minutes and knocked again. The whole area was of leafy tranquillity. Very naff. I wasn't sure what to do. It had cost me a bloody fortune getting here. I thought I'd just check round the back. The sound of a low aircraft made me glance up, and for a moment I thought I saw a face at a window. I could have imagined it, but why would I? I banged at the back door and shouted.

'Professor Hartley, my name is Keith MacNab. I need to talk to . . .'

The sudden shrill blast of an alarm rang straight through me. Damn, damn, damn. Time to go. I sprinted back along the gravel and came out on the pavement just as a police car pulled up. Oh shit. My first instinct was to run, but I steadied myself. I hadn't actually done anything wrong.

'Want a lift, sonny?'

Oh God save me from the sarky copper.

When I phoned home from the police station I prayed it would be Mam who answered. It was Da.

'Da, it's Keith. I'm at the police station, in Bristol. I need you to come and pick me up.'

'No fucking chance: it was two–nil at the first half. I'll get your mother, hang on.' There was a silence and then Mam came on the line. 'Keith, that you? Where are you? I've been worried sick.'

I was faintly embarrassed when my mother turned up at the police station. She'd forgotten to take her apron off and she was covered in blood, or ketchup or something. She listened as the officer explained that I had been arrested for stalking Hartley. It was mad.

'I just wanted to see him, Mam.'

'Then why were you round the back of his house, son, and why did you run off when you saw the police car?' The officer raised his eyebrows at me. They were like two furry wet otters. 'And the taxi driver said you were behaving in an odd manner.'

Me?? The nerve of the man.

We drove home in silence, through streets that were filling up with traffic. 'That Maria's a nice girl; why don't you see more of her? Why don't you go to bed with her, do something bloody normal for a change.'

★

Next morning when I woke, my eyes wouldn't focus. Tiny swirling dots were replacing the sharp edge of the chest of drawers. I sat up, releasing a shot of adrenaline that catapulted round my body and smacked into my heart, causing me to lie down again. I stared up at the ceiling, watching the kaleidoscope of colours that changed all by themselves. I lay there for half an hour, trying to stay calm, until the colours began to fade again. I felt terrible and had to hold the banister as I walked downstairs.

*

Mam made me go into work with her, to keep me out of mischief. It wasn't so much a punishment as her being able to keep an eye on me. I sat in the front seat with a pile of brochures for the Orchard on my lap. On the glossy cover was a picture of the place in full sunshine. The motorway had been airbrushed out, as had the barbed-wire perimeter fence. A photo of a happy, laughing pensioner beamed up at me. My stomach turned over.

My first job was to prepare the breakfast trays, if you could call them that. One tea bag stretched to five cups and the jam was past its sell-by date, with white mould round the rim that you had to scrape off. I had to take these trays to all the trapped individuals that had the misfortune to reside here. The place was haunted as well, by a ghostly undertaker. People would wake up and find themselves being measured by Mr Portway, himself a resident who had died fifty-odd years ago. One old lady swore that he asked her if she wanted oak or pine, and she was so worried she would be billed in the next life that she had a heart attack and died. Mam had worked here for eleven years. She hated it. There was this unmistakable smell of urine that stayed on your clothes and in your hair.

Maria was waiting for me when I got home. She had her bike with her and I didn't take much persuading to go into the country for a ride. It was a gorgeous day. The sun was hot on our hair as we made our way to the bypass and up Gypsy Lane past Feltham Farm and along the narrow road to the back of the safari park at Longleat. We could see the giraffes in the distance, and elephants. Some small deer-like creatures with horns ran from us as we approached their pen. I could feel the stress of the last few days lift from me as Maria chatted about her plans. We rode down a steep hill and screamed together in a wild exhilaration with our feet off the pedals and our hair two feet behind us.

We made our way up to Heaven's Gate and sat on the damp grass, awed by the view. There was some kind of concert happening at Longleat and some strains of jazz drifted up to us. There was the sound of hooves on grass and a good-looking bloke on a chestnut horse trotted past. I knew he was good-looking because Maria's eyes were glued to him and she stopped listening to what I was saying. The sun went in at that point.

'Time to make a move.' I jumped up and tried to brush the grass stains from my trousers.

'Already?'

We were quiet on the way back, me with a multitude of thoughts racing through my head, Maria because she didn't know what was going through my head.

Everyone was in when we got back. Maria stayed on her bike by the gate.

'Bye then.'

'Bye.' She paused for a second and I thought she was going to say something, but then she just smiled and rode off.

It was to be a big family meal that night. I knew Mam had an announcement to make and she wanted us all there, round the table together. I wouldn't want to be in her shoes.

'You cooked that lamb, then?' Da came stomping in, rubbing his hands, Tam and Cameron trooping in behind him. They kicked their boots off into a family pile and queued at the sink. Tam leered at me. Trying to catch my eye, but I ignored him. Mam's face was red with heat from the Aga. The hob was covered in saucepans of boiling water.

'I looked through all my books, but there was nothing I fancied, so it's just with rosemary.'

'That's what it was bred to be eaten with. I don't like that fancy stuff. Can't beat a fresh bit of rosemary with roast lamb. My da used to say we were made for each other. He said that a sheep farmer couldn't marry anyone with a better name than Rosemary.'

We all laughed politely, though we had heard that joke every Sunday dinnertime for years, even when we had beef or pork.

Mam gulped nervously as she lifted a huge roasting dish from the main oven. Behind her came the rasping sound of metal on metal as Da sharpened the carving knife.

'I'll carve if you want,' Mam said very naturally, still without turning from the oven.

'Don't be daft. I grew that lamb. I'll carve it.' Da was salivating with hunger, his hands grasping the carving knife like it was his own limb.

Mam sighed and placed the roast on the table. Da's eyes closed a little, then widened. 'Where the bloody hell is it then?'

Mam gesticulated weakly at the pile of chopped-up lamb's bits in the dish. There was a terrible silence followed by: 'What the bloody hell have you done to the lamb? You've mutilated it.'

'Hardly, I've just taken it off the bone; I just let the flavour in.'

We all peered at the plate, trying to work out which bit was which. Da prodded one of the bits tentatively.

'It's bone dry, and where's the offal? You always do the kidneys. You've diced up all the best cuts. That's prime Scottish lamb, that is. Have you gone round the twist, Rosemary?'

60

'I just thought it would be different.' Mam sat down lamely.

'I don't want it to be different. I want my kidneys.'

Mam bit at her finger before standing up. 'I've pickled them. The lamb had interesting abnormalities in its bladder. It was too good to eat.'

Da exploded. He lunged over to Mam with the knife and she screamed and jumped back. He tipped out the lamb bits on to the table and sorted them with his hands. It was a disgusting sight, like a pig rooting for food, dribbling and snuffling.

Mam stood at a distance. Tears were running down her face, splashing into the saucepan of carrots she was holding for protection.

'I'm going back to nursing, properly, where I'm really needed. I'm going to Albania to work as a war nurse. I don't care what sort of a wife that makes me, or what sort of mother, but in three months I'm leaving the lot of you.'

Da let out a strangled oink and rushed at Mam. She ran into the hall and up the stairs and locked herself in the toilet. Da turned from pig to chimp, running back downstairs and bouncing round the lounge with clenched fists, smashing anything in his way.

Tam started serving the meal, scraping the meat off the table and helping himself to carrots.

'Well, that went well, then.'

I decided to go out for a while. I wandered through the town, looking at all the things in the shop windows that I would buy if I had the money. I found myself walking up Selwood Road and into Sheep Street where Maria lived. I hung about outside for a while, not sure whether to go in or not. Her parents were a bit weird. In the end the front door opened and Maria poked her head out.

'Isn't the doorbell working?'

Oh God, she'd been watching.

'No it isn't.' My voice was drowned out by a test-dong.

'Seems to be fine now. Are you coming in?'

The house was cheerful and warm. I hadn't been there for years. It was full of clutter, from bric-à-brac to heavy desks spilling with sickly-looking spider plants. One corner of the room was clear for the Buddhist altar, the butsudan, and a bowl of water – for sacred reasons, I remembered, not for the dog. From the French windows I could see Mr and Mrs Alder playing giddy-wig-wig in the garden, spinning round and round making themselves dizzy.

'Sit down then.' Maria pointed to a chair and I sat down. There was a scream from under me.

'Mind the guinea-pig.'

I retrieved the black and white bundle and it sat on my lap, looking at me.

'Mind he doesn't crap all over you. Tea?'

She came back five minutes later with two bowls of tea. She wasn't wearing shoes and her painted toenails were flaking on to the carpet.

'How's your book going?' She looked at me expectantly and I shifted in my seat.

'Oh, OK.' Why had I come? I wasn't in the mood for chatting.

'I'm glad you called.' Maria valiantly helped the conversation along, but enthusiasm was lacking in her voice. She wasn't sure why I'd come either.

'I was passing.'

We both sat looking at our fingernails while the guinea-pig vibrated against me, purring furiously.

*

There was a crash as Maria's parents fell through the door, laughing hysterically. The guinea-pig jumped off my lap in fright and I spilt my tea over my trousers. It bloody hurt.

'Oh hello, Keith. How's your mam?'

'Very well; going to Albania as part of the war effort.'

'Good for her.' They were already on their way upstairs.

'It's the IVF treatment,' Maria explained. 'They're trying for a baby. It's bad karma just having the one. They don't want to put all their eggs in one basket, so to speak.'

I felt a blush stain across my face faster than the tea on my trousers. What embarrassing parents, thank God mine didn't behave like that. I made my excuses and headed for the door. There were crashes and bangs coming from upstairs, and the bulb blew in the lounge.

The weather had changed again; I was soaked within minutes. There was a kerfuffle in the town. The local hunt had gone off scent, and forty or fifty horses with their pink-faced riders were walking in circles round the market car park. Apparently the hounds had lost the urine trail in the rain and had followed a sewer back to its source, which in this case had been the public toilets, which were literally swarming with dogs. Screaming could be heard from inside, and the sound of multiple flushing. The Master tried to calm the situation. 'It's all right. They aren't trained to kill. Try not to use the toilets any more than you have to and we'll have you out in a jiffy.'

By the pitch the screaming rose to after this statement, the sentence was probably translated as 'Don't move or they'll kill. You'll be brought out in jiffy bags.'

The hissing of four or five cisterns didn't help. One of the hounds emerged from the toilet with a pair of knickers in its mouth. The other dogs seized upon this and went in for the kill, ripping the material apart in a frenzy. The hunt servants started to drag the hounds out one by one in embarrassed silence.

'We all bring a sample.' One of the riders tried to make conversation. 'And then someone runs along scattering it everywhere, and we all gallop after it. It's rather good sport.'

An old lady waved her stick in anger. 'These toilets are for the general public.'

★

On Thursday it was Priddy sheep fair. We were all up and about at 5 a.m., penning and loading the sheep in the trailer Da had borrowed from a neighbour. Maria came as well. Tam had bumped into her in the Griffin, and invited her. There were hundreds of pens of sheep of all descriptions, and hundreds of coloured gypsy horses. The ground was thick with mud and manure, the air full of the smell of roasting pig on a spit. We unloaded the sheep and then went to have a look round. There was a funfair, and notices everywhere advising us that plain-clothes policemen were in our midst, so no drug-dealing was to take place. I recognised the gypsy family I could see from my bedroom window, with their skinny nags. The haggling was in full swing. 'Ten pounds back for good luck then, mister?'

The local pub was fit to burst with thirsty traders, everyone spilling out on to the streets with their pints and fags. Tam and Cameron went off to queue for some beer and I walked with Maria as she patted the noses of many identical horses.

'I had a good time at the pub last night,' she said from beneath the mane of a brown and white mare.

'Oh, right.'

64

'Thought I should tell you that Tam has asked me out, on a sort of date. I thought you wouldn't mind, so I've said yeah.'

'Oh, right.'

We moved on to a pen of foals. ('Course they're weaned, mister, did it myself.')

'I mean, it's not as if there's anything going on between us, is there?' I chewed my nail. 'Because if there was I wouldn't go out with him, if you know what I mean.'

'Oh, right.'

There were many things I wanted to say, but I suggested we got some candy floss, and she said she'd see if the queue was any smaller at the pub, and so we left it at that.

The sheep had been sold for a pittance and Da was grumbling that he ought to call it a day. We all squeezed into the car and drove back to Frome. Maria sat between Tam and me while they discussed where they should go that night.

We dropped Maria off at her house and drove home. I walked to the park and sat on a swing, watching a woman scream at her kid.

'You will fucking do as I say, or I'll smash your bleeding head in, you hear me? You hear me?'

The child heard, I thought, though it didn't answer, too busy sucking its dummy. The woman strapped it in its buggy and went off. 'I won't fucking tell you again.'

I couldn't think why Maria wanted to go for a drink with Tam. She was supposed to be my friend. She knew I didn't get on with him, and that meant she shouldn't either. I let my trainers scrape on the ground as I swung and watched the sun begin to set over the west of Frome.

*

Tam spent two hours in the bathroom in readiness for the date of the century. I thought he was reading one of his porn mags, but no, he emerged a new man. I hadn't realised his hair was still blond under all that muck. I felt very sick inside as he bounded down the stairs, humming to himself.

'Don't wait up,' he called smugly as he grabbed his car keys and headed for the door.

It seemed very quiet in the house, just Mam and me.

'Want a drink, love?' She was filling the kettle and looking at me in a curious way. We sat down at the kitchen table and I felt a slight unease that I was staying in with my mother while everyone else was out having a good time. 'You're very quiet.'

I realised that we had been sitting for at least a quarter of an hour without exchanging a word.

'I'm surprised really. Why is Tam taking your girlfriend out tonight?'

'She's not my girlfriend.'

'She's mad about you, and I've seen the way you look at her. She should be your girlfriend. Don't you mind her spending the evening with Tam?'

'Is there anything on the telly later?'

'Of course you mind. It's written all over you. Why didn't you ask her out yourself?'

'I didn't think.'

'Are men just stupid or naïve and stupid? You'll lose her if you're not careful. She won't wait for ever.'

'She's seeing Tam now anyway.'

'Nonsense. People don't switch their emotions so easily. She's just trying to get you to notice her. She's not Tam's type, you know that.'

I wandered upstairs and fiddled with my telescope for a while. I scribbled down a few notes, but I wasn't in the mood really. I lay on my bed and thought about Maria. When I looked at my clock it was past eleven and Tam wasn't back. He wasn't back by one either. They must have gone to a club. I really wanted to see her, to tell her that I wanted her to go out with me, not Tam, but I wasn't sure how I should say it.

★

I woke at eight to the sound of the milk float from the dairy up the road. I went downstairs, conscious that I was still wearing yesterday's clothes. I went to Tam's door, wondering whether I should look in or not. Last time I looked in there I'd had my head kicked in for an hour. I braved it and peeped my head quickly round the door. Cameron was sleeping like a baby on the left bed. The right bed was empty, hadn't been slept in.

Mam looked up expectantly as I banged my way downstairs into the kitchen. She had a huge basket of ironing to do.

'I'm off out today. My training starts at ten, then I'll be going straight to work.'

'Where's Da?'

'Don't know, haven't seen him.'

'What time did he come in last night?'

'Da? I don't know, didn't think he did.' She hammered a crease with the iron.

'Nor did Tam.'

'Didn't he?' Mam was surprised, but hid it well. 'Do you want to come to work later? We're a pair of hands down. You could be useful.'

'Yeah, maybe.'

I went back upstairs and looked out of my window. Mrs Brownlow was tipping water over a pool of sick outside the deserted Griffin. She lived next door to the pub. She said the smell of vomit put her budgies off their seeds. She'd been out there every morning since her husband had died. Come to think of it, that's where she had been *when* her husband died. He choked to death on a mouthful of his own vomit. If only she had been there.

A wasp settled on my windowpane and walked through the open slit into my room. It injected its sting into the wood of the frame, probably bent its leg back. I hate wasps. With the edge of a magazine I knocked it into a spider's web and watched it flounder, turning over and over, getting more and more caught up in the sticky mesh until it was barely visible. The spider, alerted by the vibration, shot out of a dark corner and went to find its breakfast. I saw Tam and Maria walking hand in hand down the road. Tam stopped to stick his tongue down Maria's throat. With my magazine I squashed the pair of them. The spider and the wasp, that is.

The Americans broadcast their pictures of Mars. The BBC showed them on *News at One*. They had picked up more signals from their ultrasound equipment. How incredible it would be to be at the centre of activity. To hear the information as it was first received by satellite. Professor Hartley had been there, working at NASA. Imagine being in space, looking out at the fragile green and blue planet that we think of as the centre of the universe, just one of many planets, a marble in a full jar. Could you ever go to Woolworths for a pair of socks again, because socks are so ephemeral when you have seen the world, really seen it? The only thing I was sure of was that I didn't want to be looked at, the worm in the worm farm. I wanted to be the one looking. I had to get out of here. Maria was getting out; so was Mam. I didn't want to be the one left in, particularly me of all people, the one who most deserved to be out. I felt a deep depression settle over me.

CHAPTER SIX

It was 14th February. We were standing on Catherine Hill with hundreds of other kids, staring up at the Valentine lamp, as a man with a burning taper opened the glass door and lit the wick. Mam was holding my hand, which was mittened. Apparently after a bout of whooping cough, it was sensible to keep my hands warm. In my free hand I clutched my jam jar with my candle inside, the warmth just reaching my skin. Cameron had two jam jars, which was practically unheard of. Tam had extinguished his candle with his tongue.

The sky was black and full of clouds, the street lit by candles and shop display lights. We all sang 'Frere Jacques' and then an ambulance was called for the lady in front of us, whose skirt had caught fire. We waited until the woman was taken away then we climbed up Catherine Hill towards home, with Tam dragging me by my hair and Cameron screaming because the ambulanceman had taken away his jam jars.

'That's the last time I take the three of you anywhere,' Mam spat through gritted teeth.

★

Mam shook me awake at some unearthly hour. I was having an incredible dream that I had been the first man on the moon. I was walking on this spongy surface and there was this strong smell of mature cheddar all around me.

'Wakey wakey, time to go to work.'

'What are you talking about?'

'I've found you a job: just a couple of hours here and there for Mrs Brownlow opposite.'

'Fuck that, I'm not clearing vomit.'

'Not vomit, her garden and a few other bits and bobs. She's getting on. After poor Albert passed on she can't do it all herself.'

'Oh God.'

Mrs Brownlow was waiting for me when I eventually staggered over the road. She poked me in the ribs and exclaimed, 'You're far too skinny. Don't your mam feed you right?'

'What do you want me to do?'

'Budgies need clearing out. Come along.'

I presumed by that she meant the cage, but when she showed me the huge aviary in the conservatory I realised that she did actually mean the budgies.

'Albert used to take the dead ones out for me; I'm damned if I can catch them.'

There were two or three hundred birds in the cage. More than two-thirds of them were dead.

'I put more in when they get low. It says in my book to deep-litter them.'

'I think it meant the bedding,' I interjected, but she wasn't listening, fishing a Sainsbury's bag out of her pocket. What did she mean, she couldn't catch them?

I opened the little door of the cage and started hooking the corpses out one by one, then by the handful. The live specimens squawked in terror and flew round the cage. Some were still alive, but on their way out, so I chucked them in the bag as well. Fewer to take out next time.

It took about an hour to get down to the remnants of bedding. The aviary was lined with a bit of newspaper and as I delved around feeling for more rejects, my hands closed on a hard object. It was a bottle of stout. Good for feathers, I concluded, or beaks.

Mrs Brownlow appeared when I was finished, with my carrier bag full to brimming with the dead and the nearly dead.

'Here, son, your mam said ten was enough.'

I put out my hand for a note and a 50p landed on my palm.

'You're a good lad. There's not many that would do that for ten bob.'

I thought she was going to show me out but on her way to the front door she suddenly veered left into her lounge. On a table by one of the chairs was a glass of weak-looking squash and a plate of shortcake biscuits. She pushed me to sit down and she sat opposite, her hands limply on her lap. Damp was showing through the vile floral paper that looked as though if someone sneezed suddenly the whole lot would come down. There were photos everywhere, of herself and (presumably) Albert when they were younger. He had been a tall man, distinguished-looking. She caught me looking at the photos.

'That's my brother,' she explained. 'How I loved him! Dead now, of course. Albert could never live up to him and my goodness how he tried. That's my Albert there on the mantelpiece.'

In a tiny round frame, Albert, beaming out from a large rosebush, did not look very imposing. 'How he hated all my pictures of Charles.' She chuckled, obviously reliving some low point in her husband's life.

'What happened to your brother?' I had to ask, though to be honest I couldn't give a monkey's.

'Died of pneumonia, just after the war. Fought all these bloody Germans for his little girl, as he used to call me, then died of bloody pneumonia in some foreign hospital somewhere, never came back to me.'

I put my empty glass down, the acid drink making my teeth grate.

'Thanks for the drink. I'll be off then.'

'You haven't finished your biscuits.' Considering she'd put out an entire packet, that wasn't surprising.

'They're going stale, I'll only chuck them. I'll put them in a carrier for you.' She fished round in her pocket for another Sainsbury's bag.

'Yeah,' I thought, 'if you can catch them.'

Tam and Cameron were going shooting that night and I decided to go with them. We stopped at the offie for a couple of six-packs and some crisps and then headed up to the woods near Horningsham. It was eight o'clock, spring-dark still. We pulled over into the lay-by and unloaded the shotguns and cartridges, a large torch and the food. We all jumped as an owl hooted.

'I'll shoot that bugger if it does that again,' Tam growled, shamed by his involuntary reaction.

We made our way through the undergrowth, stumbling in the darkness where the torch missed. At last we were out in the open, on the hillside which looked over Bradd's Farm. We spread our coats on the ground and settled down. Cameron split a six-pack and handed us a can each. We sat in silence as Tam loaded the guns. They were both presents from Da, for Tam and Cameron's twenty-first birthdays. The torch lit the valley with a pale ghostly light. The moon slipped out from behind a cloud and added her own silver diffusion to the sky. I sat, straining my neck, counting stars, the adrenaline pumping through my body. This is astronomy, I said to myself. When you take away the telescope, this is the reason why and how, the relationship between stars and planets and us. And them, if there is life in space. I felt an overwhelming sense of saneness.

A crack and a flash blasted past me and I leapt in the air. Shit. A hundred yards away a rabbit lay twitching, its back leg rotating as if it was still running. I gulped at my can of drink. Cameron threw a packet of crisps in my lap.

'Cheese and onion all right?'

There was another blast. I couldn't even see what had been hit, but by the whoops from Tam, I knew something had been.

'Pheasant.' Tam enlarged upon his kill. 'Fucking feathers flew sky-high. Chuck a can over, Kathy.'

I hated my nickname; Da's idea.

Cameron took over. He wasn't such a good shot as Tam – wasn't such a good anything really. It struck me as I watched his profile how little I knew my brother. He wasn't one for conversation. He worshipped Tam, wanted to be everything Tam was, and he was a Tam in miniature, a Tam in the making.

Cameron pulled the shotgun into his lap. 'Would you fucking believe that cat?'

A large black farm cat, not the slightest bit perturbed by our presence, had sneaked down and was edging away with Tam's big buck rabbit in its mouth. The rabbit was much too heavy:

the cat could barely lock its jaw round the rabbit's neck. Cameron took aim. He let the cat get a few paces away, let him get his confidence up, let him stop for breath to renew his grip. And then he squeezed the trigger. The cat fell instantly. In the dark it was hard to tell the two bodies apart, their limbs so entangled. Tam and Cameron fell about laughing. I felt a bit sick – probably the drink.

It was past midnight when we got in. Da was sitting reading the paper with a large glass of whisky in front of him. Tam and Cameron pulled out chairs and sat down, leaving me to grab some glasses. Da looked pleased.

'All boys together then, son. Good night, was it?'

'It was all right, yeah.' Tam glugged down his dram and poured another.

'I'm proud of you, sons.' Da was swollen with pride. 'I bet Johnny Harvey's boys are at the pictures, and Eddie Smith's out with girls or the like; you're real "boys boys", you are. I'm dead proud of you.'

His pride even included me, I noticed, a rare acknowledgment of my existence. I felt warm inside. The red patches on Da's cheeks proved it was the drink talking, rather than a major personality transfer, but I felt that something had been achieved that night. Shame about the cat though.

★

The next day things were back to normal. As I walked into the kitchen in my Superman pyjamas, a fist came out to meet me, the impact pushing me backwards into the door.

'Ow.'

'Don't make so much bloody noise. I'm not asking you, I'm telling you.'

Da's face was scrunched up, broken blood vessels leaking under his eyeballs. He smelt of stale alcohol and cigars and looked about ninety. I put the kettle on, cradling my face. This seemed to inflame Da some more.

'Stop acting up, you bloody little cunt, you pile of shit, you . . .'

I didn't want a repeat of Da's upper cut at its finest, so I ducked round the table and back upstairs, bloody fast.

'And where's your bloody mam? Should be going down the shops for simple things like painkillers, instead of playing Florence Nightingale to a load of stinking foreigners.'

I guessed that the ibuprofen still hadn't been replaced, and that Mam had gone to another training session.

I caught the bus into town. Old ladies clutched their handbags to their bodies as I squeezed past looking for a seat. It was my face, I concluded, or what Da had done to it. My cheek was twice the size it should have been and one eye felt as if it was being pulled downwards. I opened a packet of crisps and read the graffiti on the seat in front of me. One of my front teeth moved as I ate, but I knew it would cement itself in again, so I wasn't too worried. There was a TO LET sign outside the scientific-equipment shop up Catherine Hill, a piece of hard-board covering the front window, which had obviously had a brick through it at one point. There were several empty shop units at this end of town. I bought a Cornish pasty from the baker at lunchtime and sat on a seat in the car park, next to a drunken woman who kept calling me Bella. I found a piece of metal in the pasty so I chucked it in the bin. When I walked off, I saw the woman fish it out again.

*

Mam had her shoes in her hand as she let herself in the front door and collapsed on the chair in the lounge.

'Where is everyone?'

'Out'

'Oh right.' She looked whacked.

'Do you want a cup of tea?' I hated making tea.

'I kept going over and over it. I just couldn't remember how many milligrams of morphine I should give in this case study.'

Her face was completely drained of expression, her voice empty. She sighed and pulled herself out of the chair and wandered into the kitchen. She peered into the empty fridge.

'Too much to hope that someone else would do some shopping I suppose?' She found a tin of ravioli in the pantry and opened it.

'I don't suppose you know when your da's getting home?'

'I didn't ask; he had a hangover.'

Mam raised her eyes to the ceiling, with a God-help-me look.

'And are your brothers going to keep a low profile as well?'

'I expect they're at the pub. I think Tam's meeting Maria.'

Mam looked up from what she was doing. 'And how do you feel about that?'

'I haven't thought anything about it.'

'I thought you two were getting on well?'

'We are. We're mates.'

Mam pursed her lips and put the grill on. I made my escape.

My bedroom was in a state, clothes and papers everywhere. I could hardly open the door to get in. Of course, Mam had been at her training, so the bed was still unmade, with the tea stain over the duvet and crumbs inside the pillow. This is the future, I thought to myself, when she goes. I found the radio and switched it on. The clipped accent of the announcer burst into the room.

'The current sci-fi craze has hit new heights. More books and videos have been bought on the subject than ever before. Television schedulers are queuing up to buy the latest space film releases, in what has got to be the event of the century. We are still waiting to hear the results of the tests carried out on the surface of Mars, and so we'll play you out with the Carpenters, "Calling Occupants . . ."'

At about eleven o'clock I went to bed, sick of hearing the sound of laughter coming from the Griffin. It must have been about midnight when a loud explosion woke me. I sat up and pulled back the curtain to see the most incredible firework display of my life. Rockets were hammering out into the night in all directions. There was a red glow to the sky, like the reflection of fire. The fireworks factory must have gone up. I tried to focus my eyes, which were rebelling for want of sleep. The sound of fire engines could be heard in the distance. I watched the oranges, reds and greens flashing into the night, accompanied by the panicked baaing of several hundred start-led sheep.

I must have fallen asleep shortly after, because when I woke it was light, with the cloaky smell of gunpowder heavy in the air and the sheep grazing peacefully on the hillside.

Mam was full of it when I stumbled downstairs.

'Did you hear that explosion? You'll never guess, the fireworks factory was torched. Arson. It's in all the papers.'

'Oh right, Any cereal?'

'Sorry, love. Tam finished it earlier.'

78

The doorbell rang.

'Can you get that, love?'

I hated answering the door. It was Maria, standing on the step.

'Hi.'

'Hi.' I echoed

She scratched nervously at her arm. There was an awkward silence.

'How are you?'

I didn't want to do this, because as far as I was concerned she wasn't my friend anymore.

'Fine.' I shifted awkwardly.

A shape appeared from behind me.

'All right? Let's go then.' Tam pushed past, his elbow catching my rib.

'Bye, Keith.' Maria smiled as Tam put his arm round her shoulders and escorted her off to God knows where. It took me about five minutes to realise that I was still standing there, like an idiot.

Mam collared me to go round Sainsbury's with her, and as I had no job or girlfriend or career to think of, it was that or stay in a bed that needed changing. The road was busy up to the roundabout. Three separate strings of racehorses passed us, holding up the traffic in the opposite direction, lorries lining up like carriages on a train. We parked up in our usual spot, three from the left under the trees, and I noticed that next to us was the same car that always parks in the fourth space from the left, and I realised why Mam was leaving. I didn't blame her for wanting to escape the monotony of living somewhere too long. I couldn't imagine spending the rest of my life here, next to the brown Ford Escort. Another thing, I couldn't get Maria out of my head. The fact that she and Tam were rapidly becoming an item was hard to accept.

When we got home Maria and Tam were drinking tea in the kitchen, their legs touching under the table. I tried to bolt upstairs, but Mam grabbed my arm, reminding me that I was carrying four fit-to-burst carriers. On cue, one did burst. A four pack of stripy-packet baked beans hit the lino, crushing a box of tampons in their path. Tam nearly choked when he saw them.

'Super absorbent? Not your usual brand, Kathy.'

All the blood in my body galloped to my cheeks, which throbbed tightly with embarrassment. Maria, I am sure, had a grin on her face as she disappeared under the table in search of the beans.

'My Mum says these are just as nice as Heinz, you'd never notice the difference. She keeps meaning to buy some.'

My blush took on a new dimension. Oh God, we looked really scabby, buying the stripy special offers rather than the brand names. I presumed all mams did this. Apparently not.

Tam picked his keys off the table. 'Come on, let's go.'

Maria reappeared with two more cans, which she placed helpfully on the table. 'Nice to see you, Mrs MacNab, Keith.'

I didn't look at her. I was busy searching for a tin that wasn't there, so that I wouldn't have to pick up the tampons.

'You should have asked her over to the pub later for a drink.' Mam put her bags up on the table and started unpacking them. 'Damn.' She smacked her forehead in punishment. 'I forgot the bloody ibuprofen.'

There was the sound of a key in the lock and Cameron and Da came in, both up to their eyes in mud.

'For goodness' sake, change in here.' Mam looked at the trail that followed them.

'Where's Tam?' Cameron undid his laces.

★

Mrs Brownlow put a note through my door next morning. Could I possibly go round and trim her hedge, 'because ever since poor Albert died . . .' She was waiting as I crossed the road and opened the little gate that led to the back garden. She had a shovel in her hand and I knew she had been clearing vomit again. I could smell it in the air and as I lifted the lid of her bin to throw a sweet wrapper inside, it was there. The stench was appalling; it brought tears to my eyes. Mrs Brownlow grabbed the lid from me, doubling her height in her anger. 'Don't touch my lid, don't ever touch my lid,' she yelled as if I'd committed the most indecent act of sexual violence ever. Bloody hell, poor Albert was best out of it.

She shrank down again. 'Can you start on the privet? It grows so fast this time of year, loses its shape so quickly.' She pointed to a pair of hedge cutters and I started the monotonous task of chopping and trimming. Mrs Brownlow stood, hands on hips, watching me. 'You missed a bit. Bit straighter there. Back a bit.'

After half an hour she went inside and let me get on with it. The garden was very overgrown, as if it had died with Albert. The layout was organised, but the beds were full of rotting dead flowers and nothing seemed to be growing, except for the hedges, though the earth was black and crumbly. An empty can of weedkiller abandoned on the grass made me wonder whether the flowers and plants had in fact been poisoned. Perhaps she didn't realise that weedkiller killed flowers too.

At about twelve o'clock she brought me out a tray of chicken sandwiches and a glass of milk. 'That will put hairs on your chest,' she said, rubbing my chest with her cold hand. I thought of the money and tucked in, not flinching when her fingers pinched a fold of skin. 'What's your mother playing at, don't she feed you right?'

I was finished by four. The hedge was looking straight and I'd swept up. Mrs Brownlow was on the phone and so I chucked the remaining sandwiches in the forbidden bin. As I closed the lid I caught sight of a pile of old photos. I racked my brains, but I couldn't for the life of me remember whether the man in the pictures was poor Albert, or the brother. What did it matter anyway? I closed the lid quietly and finished my drink. Mrs Brownlow gave me five pounds which was a bit more like it. She let me go on the promise I'd come again next week to start on the borders.

I went for a walk before I went home, up Keyford Street, where the farrier was shoeing a couple of gypsy horses. The farrier, Ed, was shaking his head as he hammered a nail into the foot of the black and white pony that was often tied up outside the Beehive. The gypsy was trying to sell Ed back the anvil that had been stolen from him the week before.

'I tell you, it's mine; look, my initials are on it.'

'Can't be yours, mister, this anvil belonged to my father's father, fifty quid I'll sell it you.'

When I got home Mam was reading the papers over a cup of coffee.

'It's awful' she said without looking up, 'another school has been hit in Helstad. They're still digging through the rubble for bodies.'

'Is there any bread?' The bag on the side was empty.

'In the cupboard. No, the other one.'

I made myself two rounds of cheese and banana sandwiches and downed them with a pint of milk and a bowl of ice-cream. Mam looked up disapprovingly.

'I hope you're going to look after yourself when I'm not here – eating properly, I mean, stuff like that. Clean underpants don't grow on trees either. They have to be washed and dried same as anything else. I can't help but worry about you.'

Cameron's coat was on the table in front of me. As I ate my tea I rummaged through his pockets. A folded bit of paper fell out on to the table. Just a bill for a can of petrol.

CHAPTER SEVEN

Da came stomping in the back door, kicking his boots off and showering the flagstones with dried sheep crap. Mam didn't comment on this, just shot him a glance to test what sort of mood he was in.

'Cold as hell out there today, Rosemary.' It wasn't particularly cold: he was just struggling for conversation. 'Still, summer's just round the corner.'

It was sad, two people who had spent most of their life together exchanging niceties about the weather. I'd rather they argued than that. At least you know where you are when he takes his belt to you. They had hardly exchanged two words since Mam's announcement that we weren't good enough for her any more. I watched them from the kitchen table, still talking about temperatures and frosts, and it was pitiful. Usually Mam was the peacemaker. Even after the black eye he'd given her once she had called the truce. And we had had to endure the squeaking of their marital bed for over an hour as they shagged and made up. Thank God they didn't do that sort of thing anymore.

Da was standing awkwardly, leaning against the kitchen door, smoothing his hair with his hand. He was trying, really trying, I don't know why or what for. Had he finally realised that it was him who was driving her away, or was he trying to regain some kind of control over her? Maybe a bit of both. A pause in this strained conversation made him glance over at me. 'Hello son, got a job yet?' No antagonism, an interested question. It was the second choice: he was trying to regain control.

★

We went to see a band, Tam, Cameron, Maria and me, or rather Tam and Maria, Cameron and me. I remembered the last time we had heard live music, at the rave, when Maria and I were sort of together and it made me sad. So sad that when Cameron offered me a tab of acid I took it, because it didn't matter any more. I chewed the little bit of paper that stuck to my teeth and drank more than I should have done, and it felt good this time: no underwater noises, no demons, just the pumping, beating ache of adrenaline surging in my chest, and for once there was no talk, no voice in my head, no first-person narration eating away at me. Not even the accusing face of Maria as my legs floated past my body, could get me down. I was laughing like I had never laughed before. Then I blacked out.

I don't know how much later it was, but I woke to the sensation of baked beans being poked down my throat. I was gagging, but they kept coming. I opened my eyes, expecting to see psychedelic paisley shapes, but instead there was Maria, holding a fork.

'Oh, thank God.'

I turned over and threw up a lot of liquid and beans. I half expected Mrs Brownlow to appear with her shovel and bin to clear it up. It was the racing, burping, vocal kind of vomit and I wished Maria wasn't there to hear it.

'Tam, it's all right, he's come round.'

I was on the sofa at home, though I don't know how I got there. I could feel something sticky in my trousers, that wasn't piss. Christ, that adrenaline. Tam came in, carrying a glass of orange juice.

'Vitamin C, that's what he needs to bring him down.'

'He is down.' Maria snapped, taking the glass anyway and putting it to my lips. The juice slid down my throat, taking with it the few remaining lumps of vomit that were round my teeth. There was a bit of a commotion at the door. I could hear Mam's voice.

'What the bloody hell happened to you?' She turned to Cameron, who shrugged his shoulders. Tam had disappeared. 'Not you again, Keith, of all people.' Her eyes were accusing as she turned to me. 'How could you do it, turn into a drug addict just to stop me from having a life, how could you?'

Hold on, she was taking this way too far. It was just the once. She read my mind.

'This is the second time in the space of a few weeks. What are you doing to yourself? You used to be so ambitious. I was so proud of you, and look at you.'

I felt conscious of the congealed mess in my trousers and hoped she wasn't referring to that. 'You need help, Keith, professional help. I don't know where to begin, but first thing I'm going to take you down to the surgery for a check-up, and then we'll get some leaflets.' She paused and looked up at Maria, who was still holding a fork.

'I'm surprised at you, Maria. Funny sort of friend you are, letting him get in such a state.'

Maria let out a scared-sounding sob and put the back of her hand to her mouth before running out of the room with the fork.

'She's not my friend.' I closed my eyes, but I couldn't escape the drilling that went on and on into the night, and hoped it wouldn't permanently damage my hearing.

★

The doctor's surgery was alive with posters, telling me to take drugs, to not take drugs, to use a condom, to protect pregnant mothers from rubella. There was even a poster displaying a large pair of sucking lips, informing that cold sores kill. All this information shouting at me the minute I walked in. Mam was behind me with a face so grim that it said, 'If you so much as think of bolting, I'll do more harm to you than a thousand bloody cold sores.' I sat down on a chair with no back and wondered why everyone was staring at me. An old lady leant forward and told me off for sitting on a table. I didn't know what she was on about so I ignored her. A small child was asking it's mother why she had to see the doctor, and all her attempts to change the subject didn't offset the little bulldozer.

'Is it about your sores, mummy?'

Everyone looked over with interest as the woman redid the kid's plait with force.

'Ow! You're hurting me, mummy.'

The nurse came to get me before long. She had long blonde hair in a pony-tail and was so body-pierced it was difficult to make out her face. She led me down several long corridors until we reached a little room with a table and a couch inside. The pierced nurse left me now and a huge battleaxe of a sister came in, putting on a large pair of rubber gloves.

'On the couch. There you are now, if you could just slip your trousers and pants down.'

I thought for one minute I was still dreaming, that this was some kind of erotic teenage fantasy that leaves you damp when you wake. Not that I was feeling turned on; I'd never been so scared in all my life.

She was impatient now, hurrying me. 'Come on, Mrs MacNab, nothing to be worried about.' I let her lay me down on the couch before I sat bolt upright.

'It's *Keith* MacNab.'

The sister looked at me, weighing up my excuse as if she'd heard it all before.

'You're not here for a smear test then?'

I refound Mam in the waiting room.

'I must have handed my card in instead of yours. Sorry, love.'

What concerned me was the fact the sister didn't really believe me. I could see it in her eyes. I made a mental note to stop at the barber's on the way home.

The doctor could have made a fortune for himself on TV, his chiselled face a medical success story. He was in his fifties and his charisma filled the room. I was squashed against the wall on a hard plastic seat that made the back of my knees ache. He spent a good five minutes studying my notes, saying, 'Um, um, um,' to himself at intervals, like a horse does when it sees a bucket of food. More posters leapt off the walls at me: SMOKING KILLS YOUR SPERM COUNT. A comedy vampire begging me to give blood. A giant nit under a magnifying glass. 'I don't think I've seen you since you had those boils on your bottom when you were twelve. Your mother must have done a good job with you. You've grown into a fine young man.' Oh God, I hoped he wasn't gay. No, he couldn't be gay, not if it was true what Tam said about them having an affair when Mam had worked part-time at the surgery all those years ago. They had been very good friends until Da got jealous about all the overtime and she'd been made to look for a job elsewhere. That's why she hadn't come in with me, she didn't want to see him. Because she was embarrassed, or she didn't want to awaken old ghosts? Or because he was a complete arse? I don't know.

'How are the boils then, that cream do the trick?'

I nodded. Course they were better. I wouldn't go six bloody years with fifteen great boils on my backside, would I?

'Not a bad record is it, Keith, no major infections or anything . . .'

'I stayed clear of infections because I don't have many friends.' I thought it best to point that out.

The doctor smiled, condescending, his head on one side like one of Mrs Brownlow's live budgies.

'Your mother, Rosie . . .'

Rosemary, R–O–S–E–M–A–R–Y.

'. . . tells me that you have started to dabble with substances. Well, my advice is give up, clean up and get yourself a girlfriend.' He paused, like an American president, waiting for an applause.

And that was it, the big speech. Maybe Da had been right to smash his car up all those years ago.

When I found Mam again, down by the coffee machine, she looked up expectantly.

'Well, what did he say?'

'He said I was absolutely fine, and that I should eat more greens.'

The tension drained from Mam's face. 'Oh I'm so glad you went to see Julian. He's put my mind at rest.'

*

I thought at first that I had walked into a women's hairdresser, because of all the pictures of girls everywhere. Even the magazines were full of women's hairstyles, which I thought was odd till I realised that the models were naked.

'Want to come this way, dear?' The proprietor, Henry James, stood with hands on hips, and it reminded me of an actual dream I'd had that I was ashamed to remember. I sat in the chair as if it was electric. This was a momentous occasion. The final but one transition from boyhood to manhood. The curly ringlets had to go.

'Number-one cut.'

The clippers whirled over my head as I stared in the mirror. Staring but not looking. For every inch of hair that spun up and round and down, I was losing a bit of my past. I made myself look at the emerging shape of my head, quite a bloody funny shape actually. I panicked, jumped out of my seat and pulled the towel from my neck.

'That's enough.'

The barber couldn't hear me over the noise of the clippers, so he turned them off.

'I'll leave it there, thank you. How much do I owe you?'

'Don't be daft, son, you look like a bird that's been got by a cat.'

'My head's the wrong shape for this. Fuck, what have I done? I look like a fucking billiard ball.'

'Eh, eh, cut the language, son; I know your Mam, remember.'

He held up a small round mirror and showed me the half-done back of my head. With a heavy heart I sat back down on the edge of the seat.

'Well, just tidy it up a bit will you?'

When I walked out back into the High Street, I realised

that, if hair holds memory, I'd left my whole bloody childhood on the lino, to be swept up and binned. I pulled my collar up, tucked my head down and headed home.

'How much did that cost you? Da could have done it for nowt.'

Tam's whole face wrinkled with amusement. Christ, he even stopped looking at the football to survey me. He and Da were in the lounge, watching some game or other. Tam was dribbling milk from his cornflakes down his chin; Da was looking for a peanut he'd dropped under the settee.

'Bloody hell, Kathy, never realised what a funny-shaped head you've got.'

Da held up his rescued peanut and burst into a raucous fit of laughter. 'Snap! Didn't they offer to dry-roast you as well, boy?'

'I always said he was nuts, didn't I, Da, running round with a bit of skirt like Maria without getting it on with her.'

They almost wet themselves in their hysteria. Da was clutching his chest, unable to laugh and breathe at the same time. Tam just hinged his head back and screeched rhythmically. I retreated, a round of nut jokes firing at my back.

Mam was in the kitchen; she was always in the kitchen these days. This had become her territory; Da had collared the lounge. She was reading through a thick medical journal, reeling off lists of names that I didn't understand.

★

The postman knocked early next morning. I bounded down the stairs two at a time and saw through the frosted glass the red, puffy face of Arthur. I opened the door to the sound of wheezing and the puff of an asthma spray.

'Ahh, that's better, son, thought I was a goner for a minute.' He took a cigarette from behind his ear and lit it with a lighter he took from behind his other ear. He inhaled, savoured, and then exhaled. 'Ahh, that's better, son, thought I was a goner for a minute.' He didn't seem to realise he had repeated himself. 'Nothing for you, son, just a dirty catalogue for your brother.' He handed me an ash-flecked envelope. As I turned on my heel and dropped the envelope on the telephone table, Mam came out into the hall.

'Hello, Arthur, how's the cough? You haven't cut down, I see.'

'My first one today, honest, Rosemary. I'm doing my bit.'

'How's Victor, is he out?'

I went upstairs and shut my bedroom door to cut out two boring, wasted lives. For some reason I was still hoping to hear from Hartley. I had heard from the police that he had dropped the charges against me, but I really hoped he would have given the matter some more thought, because if he didn't, that was it: my escape route from this hellhole blocked for ever. I took out a razor that was in my drawer and sat down in front of the mirror. I couldn't stay here, stuck in Frome with Da, Tam and Cameron, no job, no qualifications, no girlfriend.

I didn't notice anything as the razor slit through the top layer of skin. I had to push it in much harder. I thought something was happening as I felt a rush of blood slam up into my head, thought it should have been lower though, sort of from under the razor. Maybe you didn't die from bleeding to death, you died because you cut the circuit, interrupted the flow, like one of those circuit boards they give you at school when you're too stupid to do physics. I watched the line of blood run along my arm and drip rhythmically on to the carpet. I counted the drops, twenty-five, twenty-six, how many would there be before I was sinking on to the floor? The drips were spacing themselves now, thirty-one . . . thirty-two . . . bugger. I sneaked a glance at the head in the mirror, trying to catch him out, but he blinked back at me, and then I saw the reflection of my cut wrist, the blood dripping on to the beige carpet, and a nauseous feeling swept over me, and another rush of blood leapt into my head, and the last thing I remembered was 09:18 on my alarm clock.

The next thing I remembered was 09:19 on my alarm clock. And it occurred to me that I hadn't died but fainted, at the sight of the blood in the mirror. Oh well, I felt a bit better now anyway. I put a plaster over my wrist and went down for breakfast.

'. . . Well, give him my love, and Eileen. Bye, Arthur.'

The front door slammed shut.

I realised as I was pouring the orange juice that my pyjama trousers were splattered with bright red dots. I wondered if Mam would notice.

'I've a hundred and one things to do today. My first exam's at ten, then I've another at two. I think it's the theory first, but I'll have to check – I should have checked last night – got to pick up a skirt from the dry cleaner's on the way home, and do some food-shopping, but I should be back about six. If you could start the ball rolling for tea I'd be grateful, chuck some potatoes in to bake or something. I don't care who does it as long as it's done; anyway, I've got to go, wish me luck.' She bent down to kiss the top of my head, and as she turned to walk out of the door I noticed a spot of red on her cream skirt.

Tam came into the kitchen as the front door slammed.

'Was that Mam?' he asked somewhat unnecessarily, eyeing my pyjamas.

'You started your period then, Kathy?'

The day stretched out in front of me. It was pissing down, drumming on the perspex over the back door. I decided to walk into town, mainly because Tam had put the CD player on, some awful record by Tina Turner. The streets were running with water, little rivulets joining streams and turning into rivers. It always rained like this in spring, and in winter, autumn and summer. Our house didn't flood though, like the ones in Keyford. We were on the edge of the hill and the water hardly touched us. A couple of days of torrential rain and fifty or sixty families would be baling muddy water from their homes. I used to like to sit up by the river and will it to rain harder, so that the banks would burst and flood the little parade of shops further up. We never shopped there; it was mainly for the council tenants in the three concrete tower blocks opposite.

I was concentrating on the lines on the pavement when I collided with a woman. She was in her thirties, sitting down in the middle of the pavement, holding her head, with two Spar bags rolling round her ankles. I think she must have been standing when I pushed her.

'Oh fucking hell, look at the state of me.'

'Sorry.'

'Not half as sorry as I am. Give us a hand.'

She stood there, brushing off the wet that clung to her skirt, which was sticking to her legs. I found it difficult to take my eyes away. It looked kind of sexy, the mud and rain staining the black material, making it go all clingy. She paused, watching me watching her.

'Give us a hand with the bags, will you? I've scraped my

hands.' She had as well, mud and blood gathering round the tiny lines in her palms.

It seemed logical to go back to her flat with her, even though she carried her bags and I followed along behind. I went because she suggested it. We crossed the road opposite the little parade of shops and headed for the biggest block of council concrete. There was a strong smell of piss on the stairs and lines and patterns of colour daubed on the walls. 'Dannie loves Sally,' I read out, half to myself.

'That's "Debbie loves Sally." They live next door but one. Nice girls.'

We could see the parade of shops from the window, as the woman peeled off her wet coat.

'Godsend, those shops, I'm stuck without a car.'

I felt a pinprick of guilt. The flat was shabby, really scabby, with scratched furniture and clothes drying on a chair in the corner. A small gas oven was covered in the remnants of ten or twenty meals, and there was a smell of unwashed knickers pervading the place.

'What's your name?'

'Keith.'

'I'm Shona. Whisky?' She undid the top with her teeth and poured out two full glasses.

I sneaked a look at her. She had large bloodshot eyes and her hair was too short, the sort of hair you can run your hand through easily when harassed. She emptied her glass. 'God, I needed that.'

She undid the zip on her clinging skirt and let it drop to the ground. I felt a slight sense of disappointment at the sight of white knickers and tan tights. She was chatting conversationally as she removed her top.

'I was lucky to get this place – all because of the social. After my baby died I could have been homeless; I was in no fit state to work, what with the drinking and Ian leaving me.' She spoke with a faint Scottish accent and a strong slur. She undid her bra and I kept my gaze on the whisky glass in my hand. 'I'm an alcoholic nymphomaniac, I drink and I shag and I cry – that's the depression. My doctor says I'm doing well, and I'm making progress, though I know I'm never going to be a hundred per cent.'

A slow feeling of panic began to sweep over me. I didn't want this. I thought of Tam and cringed; no one must ever know about this. I thought of Maria in her clean clothes, the smell of shampoo and soap wafting round her. Shona stumbled and fell half on me. She smelt of old beer, the way you do when it seeps through your pores. She found the zip on my trousers and began to pull it down, her hand pushing through the growing gap. I was going hard, despite myself. I fixed my gaze on a packet on the stained coffee table next to me. It was a treatment for cystitis. I racked my brains trying to remember whether it was sexually transmitted or not.

When I got home I showered for half an hour and then lay on my bed, trying to blot out all trace of Shona from my mind. It was something I needed to practise though, I thought to myself, because it didn't take as long as it did in films.

★

The next day it was still raining. I wandered round town again, popped into the little shop on the corner for a packet of crisps and a jelly rat. Victor was out of hospital now. He was half the man he was, literally, his skin hanging in folds on his arms where the fat used to be. I supposed his skin would shrink in time. He was at a loose end, almost shifty in his countenance. The doctor had banned him from reading any of the women's magazines which had been a contributory factor to his heart attack. Now when he flicked through an *Automobile Weekly* he *was* looking at the cars.

I wandered out on to the street again, past Woolworths and the shoe shop. Before I knew it I was climbing the pissy steps of concrete up to flat 21. I knocked at the door. I could hear a baby crying downstairs. I was about to give up when the door opened and Shona looked out blearily. She was still in a pair of tatty satin pyjamas and looked dreadful.

'Oh hi. Didn't expect to see you again.'

She opened the door wider and I squeezed past her into the squalid flat. She padded after me in a pair of furry dog slippers.

'Whisky?'

I sat down on the frayed chair and looked around. Shona's knickers and tights were still in a ball on the floor from yesterday. They smelt a bit fishy. She lit a fag and handed me my drink. She really did look atrocious. Her eyes were nearly closed shut, puffy and raw-looking; her skin was dry and sallow.

'This isn't a good day for me, Steven.'

'Keith.'

'What?'

'Keith.'

'Oh, right, mornings are never too good, really. I hear that baby downstairs and I can't get Crawford out of my head.'

I thought for a minute she was talking about Michael Crawford, Mam's favourite, and then I remembered the dead baby.

'It's been two years now, and I still wake up at two and four to give him his bottle. Used to curse him at the time, but

I fucking miss him now.' She was sniffing noisily, hugging her arms round herself and drawing her legs up to her chin. I put my drink down and let myself out. Shona didn't notice. I felt sick inside. And disappointed. I'd hoped to get a bit more of what I'd got last night. This made me feel even more like shit than I did already.

I passed Maria on the way home. Her hair was sleek and shiny despite the rain, and her skin looked so bloody fresh and young.

'Hi, Keith, how are you?'

'Hi, fine.'

'Where have you been?' She fell into step next to me.

'To see a friend.'

'Anyone I know?'

'No.'

'Oh.' She looked hurt that I hadn't elaborated. 'It is all right between us still, isn't it, because of Tam? I know you don't get on with him, but it's all front. He's all right on his own.'

'I'm very happy for the both of you. Anyway, nice talking to you.'

I turned sharp left and walked up an unfamiliar street. I glanced round and Maria was watching me, confused and hurt. Well, bugger her really, I wasn't in the mood for hearing what a great guy my brother was. They all said that, till he got what he wanted and dumped them, but first they always felt they had to act as peacemakers, like a bunch of bloody delegates from the UN.

At home I sat in front of the mirror in my bedroom and stared at the person looking back at me. With the shaven head, and the stinging wrists, the smell of whisky, I didn't recognise myself at all.'

I wandered downstairs and looked through the cupboards in the kitchen, but we were reduced to jam and water biscuits again, so I didn't bother. I went into the lounge. It wasn't a place I went in often these days. I tended to gravitate more towards the kitchen, which was like the faintly beating heart of a dying person, the warmth extending weakly to the limbs, not reaching the extremities. The lounge badly needed a hoover – it looked as if the monkeys of Longleat had had a peanut fight – and there were several empty cans lying about, the remnants of last night's game.

Cameron's coat was sprawled over the sofa and, out of boredom, I went through his pockets again, trying to find something that meant I could get one over on him. But when I did I went cold inside.

★

I slept in late next morning, Sunday. Mam had a friend in for coffee, one of those horrendous ones that interrogate you and ask if you have a girlfriend when they know you haven't. They were discussing corporal punishment as I crept downstairs.

'I always thought a smack on the head was very effective when my kids were little. Of course you can't get away with that nowadays.'

'That's right, a smack on the leg isn't half as satisfying, too many layers of clothes to get through.'

'And what's the good of smacking their hands? They don't feel that at all.'

I didn't have anywhere to go, so I slipped out the front and round the back to the garden. I found Da there, potting some seedlings.

'Doreen still in, is she? I don't see why Mam can't have her friends in during the week, when I'm working. Sunday's my only day off.'

Da didn't like Mam having friends any day of the week. It was a known fact. I leant awkwardly against the brick wall and watched Da's big rough hands carefully ease a tiny seedling out of its tray and into a pot. He gently pushed compost down all around it before moving on to the next. He noticed me watching him and he looked away quickly, as if he'd been caught out.

'My da used to have green fingers. Not with veggies and stuff, but with flowers. I used to spend hours watching him potting.'

'What happened to him?'

Da rarely mentioned his dad. I presumed they didn't get on.

'He died when I was nine. He was throwing a stick to the dog and the dog ran up to him like he always did, and he died. Doctor said it was the impact, but it was so slight he didn't even go backwards, fell forward gripping the dog. My aunt, she went mad, hysterical like, tried to pull the dog out from under him, but he was a big bloke, thirteen stone or more; dog was screaming.' Da paused, absorbed by the memory. But he quickly snapped back to the present, picking up the next pot.

'Dog was all right, didn't much like chasing sticks after that though.'

Mam poked her head out the kitchen door. 'Coast's clear, though it wouldn't have hurt you to say hello, it doesn't cost.'

I noticed yesterday's paper as I followed Da back into the house. FIRE AT DISUSED FACTORY ENDANGERS LIVES.

I took the paper and a bowl of Frosties to my bedroom. I felt uncomfortable. There'd been another receipt for a can of petrol in Cameron's pocket, and spent matches. Cameron wasn't a regular smoker, not since he had to be resuscitated at the age of twelve after puffing on a Woodbine. And there was a history of pyromania that troubled our family. Pyromania and impotence. If you didn't get the one, you were bound to get the other. Cameron wasn't impotent. At least that was reassuring, perhaps that would skip our generation, not that being good at sex was much use to someone who sat and watched the telly half the time. Cameron only ever slept with Tam's exes anyway. It was a kind of pecking-order thing.

I went for a walk in the afternoon, past Small's Farm and through the woods. Last time I had been this way it had been with Maria. I tried to shut that out, to enjoy the end of spring, before summer takes its hold and scorches the landscape. I saw the zebras really close up in their pen on the roadside. I ended up at Heaven's Gate. The whole of Longleat stretched out under me. The house, ugly but magnificent, protected by green plastic and scaffolding, some last minute repairs before the summer rush. I wanted to kick myself for not realising what I could have had, for letting it be pulled from under me. I thought of Shona. I tried not to think of Shona. I tried not to think of anything. I kept thinking about things. Shit. Sheep were scattered about on the hillside, full of foot-rot. I shouldn't have come here. It all seemed hollow by myself. Yet I'd walked up here a billion times on my own; just once with her and it wasn't the same any more. Snatches of conversation, looks, eye contact . . . I thought of sex with Shona: Her body over mine, sitting up on me, with her eyes wide open, watching the pigeons outside the window. Her lips pursed, with circles of inward pointing lines, like arrows for a smoker: 'Please insert cigarette here'. I thought of her afterwards, crying for someone else's baby, me forgotten. I thought of what it would be like with Maria. Stop thinking.

Mam was making tea when I got in.

'Want anything, love, an egg or something? You're looking ever so pale. Are you still taking your Sanatogen?'

I hadn't the heart to tell her that I had stopped taking them two years ago.

'Yeah, I'll have an egg, ta.'

'Tam and Maria are joining us for tea.'

'Right.'

We all sat round the table, Da, me, Tam, Maria and Cameron. I don't think Mam sat down at all, she was trying too hard. I didn't look at Maria throughout, though I'm sure she was looking at me, in her puzzled kind of way. Tam was hogging the conversation, making everyone except me laugh with his stories. Should be on stage. Cameron was quiet, not listening with his usual rapture, though he laughed when the others laughed, which was more than I was doing. Mam was the worst, tittering in a high-pitched warble, like a midge homing in on skin, or a daughter-in-law. Nerves, I guess. We were playing at happy-families, passing round the pepper and salt, though Mam was about to leave, Da was on the edge of a breakdown and Cameron was a pyromaniac. It was nearly convincing, though; anyone looking in could be fooled. But I wasn't.

CHAPTER EIGHT

The sun shone through my window, bounced off the lens of my telescope and filtered through the huge cobweb that hung over the pane of glass, roasting the two dead flies that were swaying in the breeze from the cracked wooden frame. We were the only house in the street not to have double glazing. It was another Monday morning. This is going to be the first day of the rest of my life, I told myself. The past is that. I felt I was hanging on a precipice. I was too far over to scramble back up. My only option was to let go, to free-fall into the sea below, trying not to get smashed to pieces on the rocks on the way. I got dressed and went to the library. On my way I saw Tam's car outside Maria's house. He hadn't come home last night.

I hadn't been to the library since it had been torched three years ago by vandals. I remembered piles and piles of books everywhere, musty, without dustcovers, small print wrapped in blue or grey cardboard outers, QUIET PLEASE notices and a librarian who looked permanently flustered even though the place was empty.

Not so now. This was library 2000, a learning vessel, with everything on a yachting theme. Sleek, streamlined, with computers on every aisle and a librarian with a pony-tail and steel-capped boots. All the books were new, with bright softback covers and chunky print. Signs saying SHOUT, AND WE'LL ALL SHOUT WITH YOU were emblazoned on every wall.

I found the careers section and began thumbing through, starting at Z and working backwards, since the only A's I could think of were abattoir assistant or ambulanceman, and there was a fat chance of me becoming an astronaut.

'Keith, long time no see.' It was Stuart Knowles from Frome College, a sort-of-sometimes mate. I vaguely remembered he used to wear short trousers up to the age of fifteen, and blue National Health specs when everyone else was in thin gold frames.

'Hi, Stu, how you doing?' I had to shout as the place was being invaded by hundreds of children, screaming and moaning. Stu in the library. Old habits die hard. It used to be reassuring that however unlucky I was with girls, Stu was far, far worse.

'Not so good, having to work a sixty-hour week at Singers to support the family.'

'Your parents? What happened to them?' I couldn't believe it, stale Stu working in a factory. He used to get As for everything.

'No, I mean *my* family, the kids.'

'Kids? How many you got then?'

'Six if you include the babby in the sling.'

Shit. He'd shagged and that was the proof. I'd shagged and I'd just got this itch that got worse when it was hot.

I went to the Griffin at lunch time. I sat in the darkest corner, away from the jukebox, with a pint and crisps. No Tam in here – not that I was looking. At about one o'clock Da came in with a couple of sheep farmers. They didn't notice me. One was holding out a handful of change and the others shaking their heads at the state of the agriculture industry, when a sheep could sell for less than a pint. I finished my drink, screwed my crisp packet into a tight ball and left quietly.

It was raining. I wandered round for a while, watching the raindrops fizz on the electricity cables, and ended up outside Maria's house. I knocked at the door, trying to work out what I could say, if anything. While I was wondering, the door opened. Maria's mam.

'Hello, Keith. Still scraping your plate into the bin I hope?' Mrs Alder had been the dinner lady at school.

'Do you still work there?' I wasn't really interested, but had to say something.

'Good God no, no time what with the IVF programme. I'm nearly forty, got to make hay while the sun shines. My husband, Brian, has taken early retirement to help his sperm count. Every little helps. Was it Maria you wanted?'

'Is she in?'

'No. I'll tell her you called, though. Look, you're all wet; stay and have a cuppa. While you're here, I can tell you all about the tests I've got to have, it will make your hair curl.'

I didn't need to say a word. I just sat on the patterned sofa drinking my decaffeinated tea, looking at the gaudy decor. She had to have her tubes blown, apparently. I thought she was going to show me them at one point, she got so animated.

At about four o'clock I excused myself and stepped back out into the rain, a new layer of dots marking my shirt. It was weird, being in Maria's house without her, chatting to her mam as if things were different, like I had a little piece of Maria that she didn't know about. I dithered on the corner of the road. I turned left and walked up to Keyford to those now-familiar slabs of concrete. I needed sex. All that talk of tubes.

There was fresh piss in the entrance hall, a big puddle of it. A few old chip papers blew about my legs from the draught where the heavy front door didn't close properly. There were twenty stairs up to Shona's flat. I could do them in eight seconds. Shona opened the door wearing an old faded pair of jeans and a thick jumper. Her heating had packed up.

'Fucking heater's on the blink again. The whole block will be out till they send someone from the council to fix it. All those babies as well, be lucky not to freeze to death. Thank God it's not the middle of fucking winter.' Shona felt the cold, on account of her having no surplus body fat. Naked, you could play piano on her ribs. She only ate on Tuesdays, and that was before twelve.

The armpits of her jumper were stained with sweat. She put her hand to her head and scratched at a nit. Her hair was full of them, and huge crawlers that dropped off during sex.

'I dug out some photos of Crawford, on the side there.' She gesticulated with her cigarette and I followed the trail of ash to the table. She poured me a whisky while I looked through a few blurred prints: a baby in its cot, in a pram, being held, real mumsy stuff. I double-took when I realised who else was in the last picture. It was Shona, but she looked different. There was a big smile on her face; her arms were almost plump. I had imagined she was thirty, thirty-five, but in these pictures she looked in her early twenties. She looked all right, whole-some even. When we had sex on the stained carpet, next to the ashtray, in my head I was shagging the photo Shona. I felt better about that. Afterwards I fixed the heater. Just a matter of changing a fuse, but I felt pleased with myself none the less. I asked Shona about the itching and she told me to get some cream from the chemist.

Tea was on the table when I got home. Beans on toast.

'Sorry, love. I didn't have time for a shop. Very healthy, though.' Mam looked at me suspiciously. 'Where have you been anyway?'

'Out.'

'I could have told you that.' Mam cut into her toast with a knife. A bean shot off the plate and landed on her lap. She was too busy looking at me to notice.

'Just with a mate.'

'You haven't got any mates. You never have had.'

'Jesus, is this an inquisition?'

'I'm just asking. You've gone all defensive, what's up with you?'

I took my plate and went upstairs. I looked back at Mam, who was eying me thoughtfully. The bean was on the floor now. 'If there was anything wrong, love, you would say?'

'No.'

'Mrs Brownlow caught me earlier, wants you to help her move some furniture, today if possible.'

Mrs Brownlow was waiting for me as I crossed the road.

'Thought you weren't coming,' she grumbled as she flattened herself against the wall to let me squeeze past into the hallway. There was a cardboard box on the stairs, full of tins of beans, soup and pineapple. A couple of mouldy swedes were sat on top.

'Can you drop that off at your old school on the way home?

It's last year's harvest festival gift. I didn't want it. I told the buggers who dropped it off that they could keep it, but blow me they just kept asking about the war.'

My old school was miles out of the way, but at least there was a chippie next door, so I could get something dripping with fat for supper. This was the only chip shop in town to still cook with lard rather than vegetable oil: well worth the walk.

I lugged furniture round the lounge for an hour, with Mrs Brownlow standing right behind me, issuing copious instructions. I noticed all the photos of her brother were gone from the room. In their place were a jubilee mug and a chipped china cat whose tail seemed to bend the wrong way. 'Need to build those muscles up.' Mrs Brownlow spat a blob of dribble into my ear as I puffed an old moth-eaten armchair from one side of the room to the other. Underneath was a thick sheet of dust and a lens from a pair of glasses. 'Well I'm blessed! I lost that during the coronation! To think it was there all that time.' She held the opaque lens up to the light to see if it was any use still. 'Can't see if it still works. Can you look for me?' After a while she made me a chicken sandwich, which I ate as she rummaged through her purse for 45 pence. I squeezed up the dark narrow doorway to the front door, Mrs Brownlow suddenly exclaimed: 'Don't forget the box,' and rubbed the side of her head, which was obviously bothering her. I felt her watching me as I made my way down the path, getting caught up in buddleia on the way. 'Perhaps you could trim that back for me next week.' I pretended not to hear.

The box was heavy, but I was still hungry. The thought of a large portion of chips and a Scotch egg kept me going up Seldon Road, along The Row, down Market Place and across

Elm Street into Orchard Way. I walked up the tarmacked path, past the board welcoming strangers into Orchard Lea Secondary School and asking them politely not to molest any of the children they might see on their travels. A group of kids were hanging round the entrance, clutching maths textbooks and discussing quantum physics. It must be hard for the school swats at going-home time, it must seem a long evening. At bell time I was out of the door like shit off a shovel.

I hadn't been to the place for years. And there had been no big send-off either, no mass burning of worn exercise books on the road outside, just a sudden realisation that the last exam was over and I could go home. The worst and best day of my life.

I wasn't sure which entrance I should use. I wanted to go through the doors round the side, like old times, but I wasn't a kid any more so I fumbled at the handle of the glass-paned doors to the reception. As I did the box, which was getter heavier by the minute, slipped from my grasp and suddenly there were tins and mouldy vegetables everywhere.

A door opened. The headmaster stood there, his hand automatically leaping to his head to rake his grey hair out of his eyes. Mr Benson squinted at me from behind his narrow specs, his hand getting up to a great rhythmic speed.

'Keith MacNab, still causing trouble?' He recognised me, despite my hair and my loss of virginity.

'Hello, sir.'

'See me in my office tomorrow before assembly, and don't be late.'

The door closed quickly, leaving a few grey hairs gently bobbing in the draught, before they settled on the carpet. He didn't even realise I had left. Two years ago.

I stacked the tins neatly back in the box and left them on

the desk of the school secretary, who was expressing milk in the toilet. (There was a sign to this effect). I turned the sign over and scribbled my own note on the back: RE HARVEST FESTIVAL BOX FOR MRS BROWNLOW, BRAZIER STREET. SHE DOESN'T WANT IT.

It was dusk by the time I got home. The evenings were definitely lengthening though: soon it would be summer. Up to last year summer had always meant a nightmare week's holiday somewhere cheap in Britain. After our stay at a holiday camp in Skegness, Mam had said never, never again. It had been terrible, five of us crushed together in a caravan the size of a pea-pod. The site had been a treeless open field surrounded by barbed wire. There were thousands of caravans, some owned, some rented, rows and rows and rows, five feet between each. And the weather. The east wind whipped straight off the sea and funnelled down each row. It could knock you off your feet if a gust hit you as you opened the door. The sea was like black ice, glassy and sheer with white crests and fronds of seaweed – or jellyfish, I suspected – tugging at your legs.

'Four hundred quid.' Da had said this every five minutes, staring out of the window and seeing only sheep that weren't there, grazing on a hillside that definitely wasn't there. 'Four hundred bloody quid. More than my whole fucking flock's worth.'

Mam would grit her teeth while trying to hoover sand off the lino. 'There's the seal sanctuary we could visit.'

'Four hundred quid and the whole county stinks of cabbages.'

Never, never again.

Cameron was off out to the pub.

'If you see Tam, tell him to come over,' he pleaded. He looked lost, as if he'd been cut in half.

'Where is he?' I already knew the answer.

'Out with lover girl, no doubt. It's getting serious.' His face looked pinched in the dim light. He was being shut out. He had been waiting for it to finish, like it always had before, but it hadn't. I knew what he was feeling. Tam rarely went with a girl more than a day or two, always lured by the thought of something better, which wasn't difficult because he always picked up real dogs. Not this time.

I thought of the matches and the receipt for petrol I had found in Cameron's pocket. Who was this a sign for? Tam, or himself? Cameron was like a shadow, dependent on the sun to exist. And it was bloody dull these days.

By ten o'clock there was no natural light left in the sky. I peered through the telescope, half-heartedly at first, and then the old excitement began to come back, the childish wonder of discovery. I looked up, not directly at the moon, but just past it, like I had read in a poem once at school, and I could see the profile of a face. Is this what Gagarin saw as he hurtled towards the moon? Did he recognise anyone? I noted the stars, and marvelled at how I was looking back in time, how these little snatches of light no longer existed yet I could see them. I thought of how that dog Laika must have felt, strapped in a tiny capsule orbiting this strange round ball it would have liked to chase, before it was poisoned or starved to death. Did it care if it was the first dog in space? Or was it pissed off it couldn't lick its own arse?

The thought of arses made me think of Maria. I was angry

with myself now. It was bloody hard shutting her out of my head. Everything I did seemed to create a link, even looking through a telescope. I cut my losses and went to bed.

I dreamt that night that Laika had given birth to a litter of puppies in space. They were driving round the universe in tiny space baskets, holding rayguns and practising tantric sex.

★

Tam didn't appear for work in the morning. Da went mad. I thought for a minute that I would be asked to help, so I slipped out and went for a walk, up to see the giraffes at Longleat. If I got desperate for money I could apply to work there. There was usually something going. Most of the kids I'd been to school with had ended up there each summer, for shit pay and shit hours. One had told me how four nuns in a Mini had stopped in the lion's enclosure to eat their sandwiches. A lioness had taken exception and bitten at the wheels of the car. The nuns watched with terror as the rest of the pride gathered round and began to drag the Mini by its tyres into the undergrowth. The nuns managed to give the alarm call by tooting their car horn to the tune of the Lord's prayer, so the story goes.

One of the workers had told me how the monkeys were fenced in with three strands of wire, only one of which was electrified, and a different wire was used each week so the monkeys didn't know which was live. The older ones would gang up and push a baby into the wire to check if it was electric or not. Maybe I could work a few shifts in the tea room. I was never that comfortable with animals.

I walked back through the beech trees, swishing through last year's rotting leaves and up to the hill fort. I walked down over the ford, which was high with spring rain, and made my way home. I was knackered. Da was in the kitchen when I got in.

'Where the bloody hell have you been? Could have done with you today.'

'I had an interview,' I lied.

'About time. Where at?'

'Longleat.'

'I've already told you, I've a mate there, one of the wardens, you don't have to ask for a job, it's yours.'

It felt like there was no choice. I had made an effort at sixteen not to end up there, and now I was pressured. I had no intention of contacting anyone about a job there, but Da was looking pleased with me and I felt I shouldn't disappoint.

'I'd rather get it on merit, Da, not because I'm in the know.'

Da snorted, but didn't comment.

But I had to do something. I was bored of waking up each day without purpose. There was still no news from Hartley about the course. The summer stretched ahead of me like a long road. Maybe in the autumn, I thought to myself. I still couldn't bear the thought of working when it was hot. There was too much to do, wait till autumn.

★

Summer hit like a burn on the back of your hand. One day there was rain, the next there was sun. It was July, the air full of the smell of roses from the garden, vibrant with humming bees and shouting from the school playing fields. Mam's course was nearly finished now: just one more month and then all she had to do was wait for a date. Tam rarely came home these days, and when he did he talked of getting a flat with Maria.

Cameron worked almost single-handedly with the sheep – Da's arthritis was getting worse. He had trouble walking up the hill to the pens. It was something he never talked about though. To Da, being capable was the be-all and end-all. The fact that he needed his hip replaced was obvious even to me. The way he walked, twisting his spine to ease the pain; drinking whisky by the bottleful to numb body and spirit. He and Mam rarely talked. There was nothing either could say to each other any more. Mam was going and that hung over all of us, as if we couldn't get on with our own lives till she was gone. We were waiting for something to happen, waiting for a pivot that would change our lives. We had no idea that that pivot wasn't Mam's flight to Albania, but something much bigger.

Mam was reading the paper as I came down for breakfast. She was shaking her head and exclaimed, 'The biggest orphanage in Albania has started turning children away to live on the streets. They can't cope with the influx. It's terrible.'

'Don't bother with tea tonight, Mam: Cameron and I are going to the pub.'

'Hmm? Oh right, it's nice you two are getting on so well.'

We weren't really. We just stuck together because neither of us had anything else. I went to the pub a couple of nights a week with Cameron, and spent a couple of afternoons at Shona's. I hadn't had the heart to leave her. I knew I should, but I was in need of human company outside the family. And she always let me in, she was there for me in a round about way. She had started to improve the way she looked, as well: had begun to shave the thick forest off her legs and started to wear make-up, though it was a laugh really. She still looked

114

shit. She was never going to look like the girl in the photo again, but at least she was trying.

I was feeling quite good about myself. My hair was starting to grow through and had softened the shape of my head. I was gaining muscle tone, growing taller, my face thinning out into maturity. I knew I should dump Shona and find myself a girlfriend I could show off, but it was so easy to pop round when I wanted sex, no formality necessary, no roses or boxes of chocolates. It wasn't love-making, just clinging together in pre-orgasm then turning away after, barely sweating, no kissing, together but completely apart. I knew I had to give it up, but at least this way it didn't hurt. Because it was sex and not love. Love made you feel like shit and never worked out. Sex was sex.

It was Friday night. The town was electric, charged with conversation as people piled through pub doorways, pausing to light a cigarette or to say all right to someone not seen since last Friday night. The air was full of the pumping rhythms of a hundred different songs, combining to create a pulse that ran through the town and everyone in it. Cameron and I walked down the road to the Griffin, the green lamps casting weird shadows on the faces inside. There was an urgency in the air, to drink, to score, to screw, before the pubs shut and the clubs opened. Maria and Tam had arrived just as we left home. They were going to a club in Trowbridge. Maria was wearing a tight black dress that made her stomach stick out. That's the thing about love, I told myself: it makes you fat. We had avoided all eye contact.

Cameron bought a round. We fed the jukebox and sat down next to it with our drinks so that the music sounded louder. Straight away I was aware I was being watched. A girl with short blonde hair was looking at me. I immediately studied my shoes. When I looked up again she was still watching, though she looked away sharply. Cameron's voice sounded distant.

'Your round, innit?' He was drinking fast, trying to blank out his day. I had barely touched my pint, but I went obediently up to the bar. The blonde girl took this as a sign and edged her stool closer. Her empty glass clattered on to the slop tray.

'Did you want another?' I didn't look at her directly.

'Yeah, all right then, a pint please.'

I hoped I had enough money on me for three pints. I counted out my change, conscious of the eyes of the barman and the girl. As I counted I was aware of the dark shadow of the three full glasses in front of me. Nine pence short. Fuck, fuck, fuck.

'Could you hang on a minute? I'll just get some more change.' I looked round wildly for Cameron, who had gone to the toilet.

The girl smiled and produced a purse from which she pulled out a ten-pence piece.

'I hate breaking into notes as well; all that loose change drives you mad.'

I nodded.

We stood in awkward silence. She was wearing a tight black top and leather trousers. She had a great arse, sort of kidney-shaped.

'Thanks for the drink. I'm Shona, by the way.'

I blew the head off my beer. It glided in a neat arc and landed on the flat chest of the girl. It couldn't be Shona, what a cruel twist of fate. I'd never known anyone called Shona before; now I knew two.

The barman turned the music up and I could feel the adrenalin pumping along to the beat. We wandered over to the dance floor that had been cleared of its tables for the night. Shona put her arms round my neck and smiled up at me. Her eyes looked so bright I wondered if she was on drugs.

The pub was crowded and hot. Cameron had vanished and more couples had joined us on the dance-floor, pushing us closer together. Shona leant forward as if to whisper something to me over the top of the music. I was surprised when I felt her lips on mine. She smelt vaguely of Persil and tasted of Fosters. She was in no hurry as her mouth parted and her tongue teased mine. She was calm, but bloody hell, I thought I was going to explode. My heart was beating so loud I could feel my eardrums bursting. I craned forward and her tongue slid round my mouth and my heart stopped. I was dead. I was alive. I had never been kissed like this before. Shona, the other Shona's, kisses were wet and clumsy, unbothered, doing what was required and nothing more. This was something else.

I didn't even hear the crash. Or the sound of broken glass. I was conscious of a thud, a squelching of metal, but it was nothing to do with me. I wasn't even aware of the way the pub was emptying, people falling out into the street to see what was going on.

'Come back to my place?' Shona was flushed and excited as she pulled away. 'Where's everyone gone?' Her eyes narrowed in surprise, causing her nose to wrinkle Even the barman had left the till unattended. We got up and went to the door. A faint draught cooled my face.

It was the sort of evening that left you feeling tired and

drained, the echo of the day's heat plastered on your face and clothes. Someone clutched my arm. They were shocked, I could hear it in their voice.

Then I noticed the car.

It was half the size it should have been. Like a concertina. It had hit the ancient stone wall (circa 1400AD) and turned on its side, its wheels still spinning. I recognised the number plate, though my mind was numb with alcohol and sex and it took me a few moments to work out whose it was. I knew I should know and then it dawned on me stupidly. It was Tam's.

Shona squeezed my arm. 'Come on, I only live up the road, we don't need to be here.'

Cameron was already there at the car, trying to open the door, but it was jammed. Someone found a crowbar and they managed to lever it open somehow. I stood idly by, vaguely aware of Shona pulling at my sleeve.

'It's my brother's car,' I heard myself explain over-rationally, and not too loudly. Just in case I was wrong. They were pulling a figure out of the car. It occurred to me that they shouldn't be moving it. Mam always said you could do more damage moving an injured person. I wanted to say this but my mouth was too dry and the words never got further than my throat. They were really having to pull. They were frantic and I could smell petrol. Someone was yelling at everyone to get back. I could see the light on at home across the road, and heard the front door open and Mam come sobbing out on to the road in bare feet. Cameron told her to go inside, but she was too hysterical to listen. Suddenly the person was freed, and was laid down like a twisted bit of rope on to the tarmac.

'It's too near,' someone else screamed. Cameron and the others were back at the car now. Cameron had climbed half through the open doorway. There was someone else there.

My body snapped to attention. Fucking hell, Maria was in there. I was at the car in an instant. She was in the passenger seat. Shocked but alive. She couldn't see or hear. Completely catatonic. It was a miracle that they managed to pull her out. The metal had squashed against her. You could see the indentations on her arm. Cameron carried her carefully over to the other side of the road. He hadn't done this with Tam. Tam had been dumped a few feet from the car. My stomach lurched. Mam was sitting there with his head in her arms. She was soaked in his blood, and smelt of earth. Cameron pulled her away. 'He's dead, Mam.'

He dragged her to the side of the road and we all moved back waiting for an explosion that didn't actually happen. Tam was on the road and the petrol mixed with blood was leaking all over the place. But it didn't blow. By the time the police, the fire engine and the ambulance had arrived, the fuel tank was empty and so was Tam.

CHAPTER NINE

I rolled over. The sheets were cold and wet and smelt of urine. My arms were covered in goosebumps. I climbed out of bed and walked quickly to the door. The landing light had been turned off. Usually it was always on at night; the meter must be low. I padded down stairs to Mam's room. I went inside.

'Mam, I'm wet.' Mam was not asleep. Da was sitting astride her. They were both naked. Mam's tits were loose and flabby, with folds of skin hanging from underneath. Da was panting and puffing like he was riding a horse in a race. They both looked up, startled, caught out. Da roared, 'Get the fuck out of here.'

Mam began to push Da off. 'He's wet, love, I'll change him.'

Da leapt off Mam and picked up his shoe.

'Coming in here in the middle of the fucking night stinking of piss. I'll teach you to wet the bloody bed, you little shite!' He came at me. He didn't bother to cover himself. He caught me on the side of my head with the thick sole. I sprang backwards and he lashed out again, catching my hand, forcing one of my fingers back. I stumbled, knew the step was behind me. It was fall or be hit. I took my chance and fell. Mam screamed as I hit the hall carpet.

★

It's amazing how good air-conditioning is. It could have been any time of year in the hospital, the only pointer being the type of flowers in each ward, a touch of reality among the high tech. Maria was awake when they finally let me in to see her, lying looking up at the ceiling on sheets that had VICTORIA CROSS stamped on each corner, in case the urge to steal them became too much. Her parents were outside, timing my visit, jealous of the time they were losing with their only daughter. Maria's gaze did not alter, her eyes glued to the cracks in the ceiling. She was completely and utterly uninjured. Not a mark on her. Not as much as a scratch or a broken nail. After extensive tests, X-rays, scans and so forth, they had put her in this private room for observation overnight. She'd had something for the shock, and some tablets to make her sleep, but she still kept staring. She made me jump when she suddenly spoke.

'Tam?'

I was never very good at this sort of thing, 'Oh, he's fine, tough as old boots, you know what he's like.' It came out in a torrent, and I couldn't stop myself from continuing. 'He'll be home in a few days.'

Shock maybe; complete wanker definitely. Maria turned her head and looked at me in amazement. I could see the strain in her face, the tautness of eyes fed up with fighting tablets.

'He's dead, Keith, haven't they told you?'

And then she was consoling me. And I had to appear to be shocked, then angry, and then I even squeezed a few tears down my face. Stupid, stupid, stupid.

I walked down the corridor in a daze. It felt as if someone had smacked me in the mouth and I was still reeling. It was the awful feeling in my gut I couldn't handle. The fact that there was no Tam hadn't registered. Da was sitting in reception, his fingers hard against his nose, shaking with the effort of not moving.

'Can we go home yet?' I could see Mam approaching down the shiny-floored hall.

'The doctor said to go home.' Mam answered my question without realising it.

Da looked up. 'And leave him here?'

On television, in medical dramas, there is always a long struggle in the operating theatre before it comes to this. There was always a chance, until the flat line signalled the credits. We had been cheated, gone from A to C bypassing B altogether. There had never been any hope, because Tam was dead as soon as the car hit the wall.

'We might as well go.' Mam plucked her coat from the back of the chair. She was still wearing slippers. There was blood on one of them.

'I'll walk.'

The night air felt warm still as Da searched his pocket for the car key. Behind us the hospital lights lit the whole road. Light pollution was terrible here. I watched them drive off, slower than usual, and began the two-mile walk back to the house. It was past two in the morning; the pubs had been closed for hours, the clubs were beginning to empty, the pulse of a friday night slowing, the adrenalin subsiding. A few drunks were dotted about, several couples in doorways, trying to keep the night alive. I wondered if the girl had got home safely. I remembered the feeling of her tongue on mine, and an overwhelming desire to display some emotion hit me.

I could see the lights on at home as I crossed the road by the Griffin. The road was yellow with the sand that was mopping up the petrol and blood. The police caution signs had gone and everything was normal again. But it was all different.

Mam was drinking tea at the kitchen table. I couldn't bring myself to look at her, though she was desperate for me to register her emotion. 'Thank God you're here.'

'Where are the others?' I put my foot on the chair and undid my laces.

'Da's gone missing. Cameron's out looking for him. Oh God, I can't stand this.' She buried her head in her folded arms.

'Maria's fine.' I didn't know what else to say. 'They're keeping her in overnight.'

No answer.

I lay in bed for hours, listening to the cars that turned at the end of the road. I felt too tired to sleep. It was like nothing had happened, I couldn't put a name to it; but something had happened. Like skittles we were all flying in different directions, while someone else counted the score.

★

The police appeared at eight o'clock the next morning. Mam answered the door.

'Mrs MacNab?' It was the same officer that had taken statements at the hospital. There was another one as well, an older one with ginger hair. He had his back to us, studying one of Da's roses, a cigarette drooping out of the side of his mouth. Mam nodded.

'I know this isn't a good time, but can you come down to the station?'

He was nervous, a vein ticking over his left eye. He was just a few years older than me. I felt I knew him from somewhere. I sat at the foot of the stairs behind Mam and watched the officer mentally conjure the chapter concerning grief from an invisible textbook. Mam's eyes cleared for a minute.

'You're Pam Clearford's boy, aren't you? She said you'd graduated. I bet she's glad you've been placed locally.'

That was where I knew him from: coffee mornings when I was little. His Action Man used to do citizen's arrests on my Action Man. He could thump hard as well.

'It's not like the Army, where you don't get the choice. I wanted to stay near Mum. She isn't so good now; the cancer's come back. She's on her third lot of treatment.'

Mam sat down suddenly on the stairs and put her hand over her face. The policeman and I watched awkwardly. The other officer was busy scraping a black dot off the stem of the rose.

Mam reminded me of Shona, crying for her baby, and I felt sick. The policeman cleared his throat slightly and addressed me.

'It's your dad. He's been arrested under the Cruelty to Animals Act. He's been charged, but he can come home now. He's not in a fit state to drive though.'

I hardly recognised Da as he was escorted to the reception area. He was leaning on the arm of the police officer for support. He was one of the strongest people I knew: nearly six feet tall and fourteen stone. He could throw a sheep's carcass over his shoulder and carry it down the hillside. He had broken one of my bones once.

'What the hell have you done, Michael?' Mam's voice was low.

The police officer took a clear plastic bag out of a drawer

and tipped the contents on to the desk. Da looked at his belongings blankly and signed where he was told to for an old crisp packet, a market ticket and a box of matches.

Da said nothing in the car. He couldn't have done so if he had tried, the way Mam was screaming at him.

'Of all the stupid, stupid things to do. What were you trying to achieve?' The accelerator pedal nearly snapped as she overtook a van delivering to the shop on the corner. Da licked his finger and rubbed at a mark on the window.

'What were you trying to achieve? Michael, are you listening to me?'

I walked with Cameron up the hill to the pens. It looked as if a bag of cotton wool balls had burst and the contents used to mop up blood.

'Fucking hell.'

There were two hundred carcasses, maybe more, littered, still. Twenty year's hard slog. What a fucking mess. We walked stunned round the field, stopping only to take a stone to the occasional sheep that was still breathing, to bash its brains out and splinter its skull. We both had blood on our hands and on our trousers.

'The RSPCA are on their way.' Cameron made me jump. 'They need to collect photo evidence. Anyone would think they're on their friggin' holidays.'

They would be compiling a case against Da, the head welfare officer informed me as the cameras started to roll. Dead pleased, they were, to find the murder weapon, a blunt axe which Da didn't normally use as the head was loose. It was sealed in clear plastic.

'They're fucking gleeful, you know,' Cameron spat.

When we were given the all-clear Cameron phoned the hunt. Within an hour a big horse lorry arrived with two kennel men and together we filled the lorry with the first load. One of them looked at me sideways and said helpfully, 'It's probably doing you good, keeping busy.'

I nodded. It looked funny when the lorry was full, like a cartoon portion of bangers and mash, with the legs as the sausages and the wool as the potato.

★

I went to see Maria the next day. I thought about it for a while before I knocked. Mrs Alder was glad to see me.

'Keith. Maria will be dead chuffed to see you. Go straight up, will you? Maria,' she yelled, 'visitor.'

It was the first time I'd seen Maria's bedroom; it was large, with two windows. The wallpaper was plain compared to downstairs. Maria obviously liked pot plants. There were five or six dotted about. Mam said you shouldn't have plants in the bedroom, because of the carbon dioxide.

Maria was lying on the bed, eyes fixed to the ceiling. I felt obliged to do the same.

'How you doing, Maria?' I wriggled to get comfortable, our shoulders just touching. I spoke directly to the ceiling.

'Thanks for coming,' Maria said to the ceiling.

We didn't say anything else. I felt myself drifting off at one point, the room was so warm. I only realised when my knee jerked and nearly hit me in the face. My thumb was in my mouth as well, I noticed. I don't know how it got there. Maria looked sideways at me and lifted her thumb to my eye level. We had identical indentations.

That afternoon we went out for a walk through East Woodlands. The tracks were muddy and rutted with hoofprints. The woods were alive with pheasants, flapping out from every bush or tree as we passed. We came out by the little church and back past the pub to the green and then up to the bypass and home.

★

The funeral was on the Friday, at St Mary's. Mam made a point of introducing us all to the vicar, who was nearly seven foot tall. His cassock only reached just below his knees and you could see grey knee-length socks underneath. He had a loud, barking voice and put us through our paces: 'All together, get up, kneel down, and up.'

Dressed in suits and with the sun hot through the windows we got up a bit of a sweat and fogged the stained glass with condensation.

Maria sat by my side through the service, her teeth chattering so hard she kept jogging my prayer book. Cameron and Da sat further along. Da had his eyes closed half the time and I thought he was asleep at one point. He was sagging. You could almost see the stuffing falling out of him. I felt I needed a bicycle pump to blow him up again, round and jolly, though of course he had never been like that anyway. We all stood up and sang 'Morning Has Broken'. The great urge to giggle at Da's cracked voice was nearly too much. I dug my nail into my palm and mouthed the words silently.

About fifty people turned out for the occasion. Many of

Da's friends came, the death of a son being a very serious matter. Some relatives appeared from Lanarkshire. They sang the hymns too loudly and drank too much at the wake.

'Would you like another drink, a vol-au-vent?' Mam was efficient and calm throughout the day. In nurse mode.

'Well, that went off OK.' Mam was clearing out the cupboard under the sink. She had already had a sort-out under the stairs. 'I think I'll start on the bathroom now, unless anyone wants some more tea?'

Da was leaning against the Aga, his elbows resting on the red enamel.

'Shouldn't have had him burnt, Rosemary, like a bloody great hunk of meat.'

Mam looked up defensively. 'How can you say that? You want him to be stuck in the ground like a bloody seed potato?'

I poured the dregs of my tea down the sink and went upstairs.

That night we woke to the sound of breaking glass. All except Mam, that is: she heard breaking glass every night as she relived the crash.

St Mary's was on fire. I could see the smoke winding round the steeple from my bedroom window. Huge yellow flames devouring the building – the Saxon nave, the medieval cross, the 1980, flat-roofed concrete extension. Roasting.

I pulled on a jumper and jeans and went out on to the street. There were lights on in every house although it was 2 a.m. I ran up to the end of the road and turned left. I had to walk back a few paces, the heat was so intense. There was a figure watching from the pavement. I recognised the rounded shoulders. First of all I thought it was Tam, but it was Cameron, his face a deep red from the fire, two thin lines down his sooty face. I didn't know how to handle this kind of emotion.

The church was collapsing now. It seemed surreal, standing here. The air alive with sparks that burnt out over our heads.

'Cameron?'

He jumped. He hadn't noticed me.

'It didn't feel fucking right in there.' His voice was cracked, raw with smoke. 'I hated that fucking vicar. I hated the way the cunt kept saying "Tom" like he was a fucking cat, you know?'

There were twenty or thirty people behind us now. I paused before putting my hand on Cameron's arm.

'Come on.'

We walked back to the house. Behind us we could hear sirens, people screaming, the sound of children being bundled out of neighbouring houses by parents not sure which way the wind was blowing. We shut them all out with the swing of the front door. As I walked into the kitchen, Cameron made for the stairs. I hung about for a bit, not sure if he would come back down or not, and then I went up myself, pulled the duvet over my head and went to sleep.

★

The insurance assessor called when everyone was out. He was a friend of the family and wanted to offer his condolences and to let Cameron know his findings. The car was a write-off. We didn't need an expert to tell us that. He was sympathetic, telling me ways in which it could have been worse. His friend had been at the scene of a crash and had seen the brains of a baby splattered all over the road. At least that hadn't happened to Tam. He could have been disembowelled or anything, according to this bloke. He talked for a long time about all the latest safety features new cars have.

'This couldn't happen now, it's just the fact that it was an old car, a tin can really. No bracing at the sides to stop it buckling in. Car accidents aren't what they used to be,' he explained quite ruefully. 'Not so much gore.'

When he went I lit a cigarette, my second that day. I didn't usually bother, but it gave me something to do. I was smoking the same brand Tam smoked. He had been a forty-a-day man. I could never get up to those dizzy heights. That was probably what had happened at the wheel of the car: lit a bloody cigarette and lost his concentration. Maria would have yelled, 'Look out', and he would have swerved to avoid a car, caught the lamppost and then hit the wall. That was as good a theory as any, because Maria couldn't remember.

They had let me see Tam at the hospital. For a minute. I went in on my own and I saw the body formerly known as Tam. He had a burn mark on his chin, hence my theory.

There was a report on the news that within ten years the whole of Scotland could be covered by a mile of ice. Birming-ham would be tolerably cold, the south just middling. Frome, of course, would just be wet. It would take a long time for the greenhouse effect to alter that. I had even known local people to petition Sainsbury's to restock CFCs. (These were generally people who had an interest in the tourist industry). There was a book I read years ago about the Antarctic, which said that fossils of palm trees had been found under the ice. It seemed to me that the world was full of extremes, nothing stable or done by half. Like you couldn't have a car accident and be hurt. You had to be dead, or to come out of hospital with barely a bruise, like Maria. When the doctor called in to see how Mam was, he said that Maria might be fine physically, but mentally she would never recover. Mam took reassurance from this.

★

Tam had been dead for a week. We were used to setting four places at the table now instead of five. Cameron no longer had to share the bedroom. Tam's bed was gone and all the furniture changed round. Da still went up to the pens every day, although they were empty. And Mam missed just one of her lectures. We wiped him out. I hadn't talked to Cameron about St Mary's. I didn't know how to broach the subject, so I chose to ignore it. And we all went about our lives as if nothing had happened.

Maria and I caught the bus to Warminster. The doctor said she should go out. She had been experiencing breathing difficulties, though there was no physical cause. We had a hot chocolate in the Gorge Cafe. The red-painted walls and ceilings were carved out of rock. We had a look round the market and then we went home again.

'Thanks for this.' Maria was referring to our outing.

'That's all right.' I studied the hole in the knee of my jeans and really, really wished that she hadn't slept with my brother.

★

Mam was tidying out the kitchen cupboards. There were saucepans everywhere. Da was in the garden, weeding the seed trays out, a little too brutally by the look of the pile of rejects. The weather was close, the house horribly still. I couldn't stay here, pretending nothing was wrong. I felt this thick depression settle over me like a pea-souper.

I popped in to see Maria again. The family were having tea and asked me to join them. They were in a jolly mood. Maria's mam had conceived at last. Maria's dad asked me how I was bearing up. 'Crashes are terrible things. I remember this crash I saw when I was a kid,' he enthused, 'this motorcyclist hit a lamppost full-force and his head came straight off and bounced over the bonnet of our car. The helmet made a hell of a dent.' Here we go I thought.

He hugged Maria tightly. 'Thank God the car didn't blow up. Here, look at this.' He went to the kitchen and came back with a bucket of petrol and a box of matches.

'Did you know, Keith, that petrol itself isn't flammable? Most people don't realise that. You could drop a lit match into this bucket and it wouldn't blow.' He was lighting the match, offering it to me. 'Go on, drop it in.'

I shrank back. The smell was filling my nose. The petrol was all over the road again.

'It's the vapour you see that's flammable; it all depends on the percentage of oxygen mixed with the fumes. Go on, try.'

I didn't say anything, I just walked out.

I went for a long walk to clear my head. Calm down, I told myself, get a grip. But it was hard to calm down when it was eighty degrees out and my T-shirt was sticking to my back. Drops of sweat were stinging my eyes and running down the sides of my nose.

It had taken three ambulancemen to lift Tam on to the stretcher. Even missing his seven pints of blood it had been a job. He must have been a good thirteen stone. I noticed he was wearing his safety boots before they swung the doors shut and drove him away.

CHAPTER TEN

The ceilidh band struck up again. The caller blew into the mike.

'Dearie me, I havnae seen such a miserable bunch of revellers since we played Lockerbie.'

It had taken seven hours to get here. Da wanted to spend some time with his family and so we drove overnight up to Carlisle and over the border. It wasn't such a squash in the back of Da's old Granada now. We didn't get crushed going round corners.

'It must be three weeks noo since you lost your wee laddie.' A pissed old lady teetered forward and gripped Mam's arm for balance. Mam nodded. It took a while for the old bat to steady herself and then she moved to Da.

'It must be three weeks noo since you lost your wee laddie.'

'Aye.' Da had regressed. He looked ridiculous in full Highland dress. He had adopted a strong Lanarkshire accent (he used to say 'Lanarksheer'). It was easier going back than forward. There was a flurry of dresses as the band struck the first bars of the 'Gay Gordons'. Mam studied her nails. They were red at the quick.

Maria had been gutted when I'd said we were going away. She was around me constantly, wanting to talk about the accident, opening her grief like a carton of milk and pouring it out. I hadn't seen either of the Shonas, hadn't had sex for two weeks. It was doing my head in.

'Walk back to the cottage with me, love.' Mam stood up.

The village was smaller than I remembered. Twenty or thirty single-storey cottages huddled in rows along different edges of hillside; white pebbled exteriors with black borders stamped around the windows. We walked in silence. The village was edged by the Lowther Hills and it was in shadow for most of the day in winter. And smothered in snow. Today had been sunny, though the air had a bite to it and I wished I had a jumper.

'I can't understand why Da wanted to come here,' Mam nibbled at her quicks. Several sheep were huddled on the road licking the tarmac.

Mam let us into our cottage. A gust of smoke let itself out. A log had fallen on to the carpet and had smouldered for several hours.

'Oh bugger. I told Cameron to put the guard across.' Mam looked at the stone floor that showed through the hole. 'This will give Alice something to moan about.' The cottage was owned by one of the 'Real MacNabs' as we knew them, the cousins who had come to Tam's funeral and sung too loudly. This was where Da had grown up. Well, in the next village.

We had been here once before, years ago. Tam and Cameron and I had climbed to the top of Suicide Hill and stood panting at the top.

'This is where people come to kill themselves.' Tam's eyes were sparkling. 'Pregnant women would walk up here and spear their illegitimate babies through their fat bellies.'

'Really?' Cameron wanted to know more.

'And virgin witches would pull up their skirts and conjure the devil to sow his seed, not knowing that his barbed cock would make them bleed to death after.' His eyes had darkened. He was savouring the thought. Cameron was hooked. I didn't bother to explain that this was where they buried those ineligible for consecrated ground, but then I would know this, I had read the tourist guide. We all lay down and after three, rolled down the hill. Tam hit the ground first.

Tam had fitted in brilliantly here. The Real MacNabs had embraced him like a son. Da burst with pride the day they got him to castrate the new lambs.

'Would you look at that, would you look at that.' Da's eyes were moist as he counted the woolly, bloodstained balls. 'Forty in eight minutes.' When Uncle Dougal had offered me a turn, Da had given me a look that said, If you show me up, I'll give you the hiding of your life. So I had shaken my head and gone indoors complaining of an umbilical hernia.

The Real MacNabs had cried real tears at the funeral.

★

'Now, Michael, what do you think of these?' Da's face was unreadable as he surveyed the pens. 'They look like a cracking flock of ewes. Do you have trouble keeping the weight on them up here?' The hillside was different from our one at home, like a bald man's head, a few weak trees straggling, swept over by the wind. The only things that moved were sheep, rabbits or grouse, giant nits that picked at the scalp. It was as if some maniac had come along with a pot of poison and wiped out the other species.

'Look at this, Keith.' Dougal unscrewed the cap of a pot of

136

poison. 'You'd be dead within seconds if one drop of this stuff touched the back of your hand.'

'Great.'

'People pay thousands of pounds to come and shoot here for a day. They come from all over the world. Think how buggered we'd be if we started losing the grouse to birds of prey or cats.'

I bought three postcards from the little sub-Post Office. They were identical and depicted sheep, tartan and heather. I also bought three boxes of shortbread biscuits, depicting sheep, tartan and heather. The woman in the shop looked at me thoughtfully.

'It must be three weeks since you loost yer brother noo?'

When I got back to the cottage I wrote the three cards out neatly. '*Wish you were here, Keith xxx.*' I addressed them to Shona, Maria and Shona respectively. I had seen the new Shona (Shona 2) a couple of times since the accident. I had bumped into her at Sainsbury's and had met her for a drink one lunchtime. She was nice. A real looker with very clean hands. I had seen Shona 1 briefly when I popped in to get my coat from her flat. She had started crying for her dead kid. And then there was Maria, who clung to me like a jellyfish in a way I had never imagined possible before she started shagging my brother.

'Women are more trouble than a whole pen of ewes and they never want it from behind.' Da's philosophy on life had some grounding in reality then.

Space. I was surrounded by space. From the top of Suicide Hill I could see at least four more ranges, all flat and low and purple, dotted with moving clumps of white. This was where sheep were dripped into Da's veins. Even if I opened my veins as wide as I could and poured and poured I would still be empty.

★

Auntie Alice took Mam and me to the Firth of Forth. We pulled up and watched a train go over the bridge, dozens of blank faces looking down into the water. Mam and Alice didn't speak much. The carpet mattered to Alice. She resorted to speaking in such a strong dialect that even Dougal had trouble interpreting.

I left them in the car park, bickering over the Highland clearances, and sat beneath the peeling paintwork of the bridge support, on oily pebbles that marked my trousers. A wet copy of the *Sun* had attached itself to the metal framework and was drying into flakes. I tried to think about Tam but there was nothing left inside my head.

Later we took a boat trip round the Forth. There was a jazz band playing on board, all crap like 'The Saints Go Marching In', that sort of shite, but no one was listening anyway, too busy watching the seals that bobbed to the surface of the water, the light causing a haze on wet fur. It was amazing, watching them roll in the water, twisting and diving. When I looked at Mam she was sobbing, her forehead against the glass of the cabin window. There was no relief from it. I felt the depression close in again.

★

Mam and I decided to go home the next day. Da and Cameron could follow on when they were ready. The MacNabs held a big drinking session in memory of Tam that night, a Viking send-off without the burning boat. There were ten different bottles of whisky laid out on the table, from Laphroaig to Glenfiddich.

'Tragic loss, Michael.' Dougal slipped the Laphroaig from its cardboard cover and filled our dram glasses one by one. 'It must be all of three weeks noo.' We were in the old parlour which stank of smoke and sheep shit. A litter of collie pups whined in the corner next to the wood stove. 'I give you Laphroaig.' Dougal adopted a sombre voice, 'A peaty taste for the return to the earth.'

Da looked down into his glass. He could see his own reflection. All the grieving was to be left here. To be put out with the dirty glasses and washed away. Tomorrow was hangover and recovery. Funny bloody lot, I thought. You wouldn't get them doing this shite back home.

★

The post had been building up on the mat, trying to climb up the door and escape back out of the letterbox. Mam binned the lot without reading it. We sat up late watching a film, about someone who gets killed in a car crash whose father axes a whole herd of cows to death and whose sister burns down Westminster Abbey. Mam sat tight-lipped all the way through.

Later I pulled down the old posters that hung in my bedroom and stood back and surveyed my handiwork. The room looked dreary. I'd forgotten that the walls were painted a pale brown. I couldn't for the life of me remember when they went from blue to shit brown. Perhaps it was the time I had my first wet dream or started secondary school. I turned the radio on. I'd hardly listened to the news since the accident. There had been no new developments in the quest to find life on Mars, just the same old stories rehashed. It occurred to me that people weren't talking about it any more. They weren't walking along looking upwards – tired of being strung along, maybe, or just not interested enough.

I tipped out my drawers on to the bed; clothes I hadn't worn for years, an old school tie, even a bag of food for the gerbil that the cat killed years ago. When this was finished I swept the shelves of my display cabinet straight into a carrier bag, all the fossils I had collected at Lyme Regis as a kid, the roman coins stolen from that shop in Baker Street by Tam and then sold to me for twice as much as the shop was charging. Like the various ages of creation, I viewed my childhood eras from the Jurassic to the modern, my evolutionary development, starting with a gold-plated milk tooth and ending with a copy of *Playboy* I'd swiped from under Tam's bed. The place was such a fucking mess, a wriggling corpse of past and present. The old Keith MacNab was in the hallway in black plastic sacks, the new one looking on naked from the top of the stairs like a skeleton that had had its flesh pecked off. It was three in the morning by the time I went to bed. Mam was still downstairs, opening the post that had been retrieved from the bin.

★

I needed a job. I'd found my NatWest statement. There was only fifty quid left of my inheritance from Auntie Fran. I'd been living off this since the spring, and now it was nearly gone. I'd got used to my days, walking through the countryside and then going to Shona's for a shag. Work had become one of those big insurmountable hurdles that hung like a wet fish in front of me, obscuring the future. Six grand. I'd got through that fast. OK a large portion of it had gone on the telescope, but the other portion had gone on cod and chips.

I phoned Maria that afternoon. She was ecstatic to hear from me and I was glad to hear her too. We chatted for half an hour about my walls and her guinea-pig. She promised to call round later with some paint. I hummed to myself as I made some toast. Within an hour Maria was at the door. Mam was in the kitchen, cleaning out the flue of the Aga which was blocked. 'You fucking bugger, you can't still be jammed.'

'Best not go in there,' I thumbed the kitchen door, 'she's going mental.' Maria laughed. As we went upstairs we could hear metal on metal as Mam hit the Aga with the shovel.

It was the first time Maria had been inside the house since Tam died. She didn't look at his bedroom door as we walked past, up to the second floor to my room.

'I could help you redecorate if you like, I'm not back at work yet. It's been nearly three weeks now.'

'I know.' I put an old Smiths album on.

Morrisey had a knack of hitting the nail where it hurt. We sat on the bed. Awkward. I was aware of a strong aching between my legs. I was confused, not sure where the boundary between sex and friendship started or finished. For interest's sake it finished when I stuck my tongue down Maria's throat. She sighed and reached for the back of my neck, her fingers pulling at my hair. Rockets were shooting up inside me, crashing into the top of my head. My knee slipped between her thighs and I could feel the warmth of her skin through my jeans. There was no messing about now. We both wanted it, but when my hand slipped up her top, she pulled away, wincing slightly.

'Shit, no Keith.' She wiped her hand over her mouth, 'We bloody can't.'

'Oh right.' I swung my legs and pretended not to care.

'That night, I finished with Tam. I told him to go and fuck someone else, because I didn't want to know.'

'I thought you couldn't remember.' I peeled off a piece of wallpaper with my thumbnail.

'You're not some substitute for your brother. It's always been you I wanted, I just didn't think you felt the same.' As she pulled the chain on her emotional toilet, I felt my desire flush away. The word 'substitute' wasn't much of a turn-on, whatever way she had meant it.

I walked Maria home. After she shut her door I wandered about for a while, chucking the odd stone at the odd lamppost, but the glass was too hard to break. In the distance I could see the concrete slab of Shona's flats rising over Keyford. Twenty or more lights shone in twenty or more living rooms. Like a moth I headed towards the lights and climbed the stained steps up to Shona's stinking flat. This time her doorway smelt of piss.

'Some fucking tom's been spraying through my letterbox.'

We had sex twice on the floor in her bathroom and then once in the bath. I helped her hang a towel rail and she made me a cup of tea, then I went home. Empty. Without the ache.

CHAPTER ELEVEN

Mam was sitting at the kitchen table opening the morning's post. She was holding a credit-card bill addressed to Tam.

'Look at this.' She held out the bit of paper and I read the columns of figures without taking them in. Mam sighed impatiently. 'I'm not making conversation; look at it properly.'

I took the paper from her. This was an account with a lot of activity. He was seriously over the limit.

'I didn't even know he had a card, did you?' Mam waited for my reaction. I didn't know he had a credit card, not with a limit of two thousand pounds which he was well over. He had missed two payments as well. The charges were going through the roof, the interest rate extortionately high. Tam had always had nice clothes. Everything had always been new. He had the almighty stereo in the bedroom, which he rarely used, and decent walking boots. Mine were full of holes. I was actually hoping to collar his boots at some point in the future. They were top-of-the-range, hardly worn, now sitting under the stairs with Mam's flip-flops and a couple of pairs of smelly trainers.

'How are we going to pay it, Keith?' Mam looked thinner than she had ever looked. She had always been quite sturdy. Not likely to blow away in the wind, Da always said. I wondered what he would say about this. Da didn't even have a bank account. He only ever dealt in cash, would refuse to take a cheque even from the market. 'Money is money,' he always said. 'You can't spend it if you haven't got it.' Tam had blasted that theory. A little bit of tarnish seemed to be appearing on the golden boy.

'I don't know what your da's going to say. We haven't got this kind of money.'

'I'll help.' The voice wasn't my own. 'I'll get a job.' I was fairly confident that Mam would say don't be daft, because I was still a kid and it wasn't my problem. But she didn't.

'Do we have to tell Da? If we could clear this between us, no one need know. He doesn't deserve this . . . Would you like an egg for your breakfast?' She tore the bill up and threw it in the Aga. I could no longer fall back on my age. It was over, that excuse.

★

The next morning I wandered down Cheap Street. I washed my muddy shoes off in the little stream that cut the pavement and opened the glass door of the job agency. Within ten minutes I had a job. The bat-faced woman behind the desk beamed at me as I filled out an application form. 'If it's factory work you're looking for, it's a bonus that you can write. You won't need help filling out your time sheets. Can you use a computer?' She tilted her head to read my comments under the IT section. 'Oh, you have a technology GCSE. We'll be able to put you on a machine in no time.'

I stepped back out into autumn drizzle a condemned man. I lit a cigarette in the doorway of the baker's. The counter girl, with buck teeth and an 'I love my Rabbit' T-shirt waved me away from the window, but I ignored her, hoping my smoke would drift through the open door and taint the cakes that I couldn't afford. Until pay-day, that is. The bat's whole face had hinged into a smile as she gave me directions to West & West, a factory in Shepton Mallet that produced speciality beers for local breweries. I was to work four nights a week, twelve-hour shifts. I was wearing Tam's sweater, one that had escaped the charity bag. It was virtually unworn, it had just a nick on the arm from where I'd caught it on a stile. The pay was crap at the factory, but it wasn't looking like I'd see much of it anyway. I stubbed my fag out on the glass window of the bakery, leaving a tiny powdery smut, tucked my head down into the neck of the jumper and walked out into the drizzle and home.

★

The factory was a huge old warehouse with twenty-foot-high doors and windows thirty foot from the ground. A minibus picked me up at twenty-past five from where St Mary's used to be. There were only two other people on board and they were taking it in turns to sniff Copydex from a paper bag. The foreman greeted me as I followed a line of people to the cloakroom and showed me where my peg was.

'You're on to a good thing with us you know.' He waited as I hung up my coat and lunchbox. He was a tiny man, barely four foot tall and he had to stand on tiptoe to undo the wrought-iron catch on the door to the factory floor. 'We're constantly expanding you know. We've had twelve new machines this month. Our productivity has quadrupled in the last six months. There are huge career opportunities coming up the whole time for a smart lad like you. This job could be the making of you.' He stared up at me and pointed to a conveyer belt where bottles of beer were running along and then smashing on to the ground. I spent the next twelve hours catching bottles before they fell and stuffing them into cardboard boxes.

It nearly killed me. Twelve hours solid, with only four short breaks, packing boxes of beer and loading pallets. The endless brown bottles on the production line marched towards me and if one got stuck for whatever reason, the bottles would explode or fall off the end, breaking in their hundreds. One of my jobs was to sweep up the broken glass. The shift started at six and the hours dragged round. The factory was too big to heat properly and I froze in my jumper. I fell asleep standing up several times, leaning against the pallets. When 6 a.m. came round with the sun I felt I had been galloped over by a herd of wild alcoholics. The minibus came at five-past and I got home as a thousand alarm clocks were sounding round Frome. The milkman handed me two pints as I wandered up the path and crashed out in the hallway. When Mam woke me at 9 a.m. I was still cuddling the milk.

I slept till two. When I woke I crawled into the bathroom and soaked for an hour. I found some clean clothes and cooked up some bacon, eggs and tomatoes. It was half-past three before I felt half-way decent again. My next shift was to start in two and a half hours.

That night was the same as the first, though the couple in the minibus had progressed to Evostick. The foreman had to wake me up at least four times. Unfortunately he would then stop to chat and his conversation was so earth-shatteringly dull it lulled me to sleep again. He was a hypochondriac, it turned out. He had had lung cancer and a brain tumour this week.

Thyroid problems last week (underactive and overactive), AIDS, a melanoma, leprosy and the flu. We stopped for a break every three hours and could either get a hot drink in the canteen or go outside for a fag, which is what I preferred to do. It was nice to sit and watch the black sky with the orange end of a cigarette warming my hands and the smoke filling my lungs. And it actually made it warmer going back inside.

★

I didn't manage to get into the country till Saturday. I slept in late, then walked up to Horningsham and then to Cley Hill. It was a beautiful clear day, not too hot. I took the steep route straight up and then in a moment of stupidity lay on the grass and rolled back down again. I felt sick for the rest of the day.

In my bedroom that afternoon I read through the notes to my book, *Observations of the Red Moon*. Chapter One looked a bit sketchy. It needed a rewrite, but it always seemed silly going back over something. Two days in the factory had made me even more determined to get on in life. I could do a rewrite, then resubmit it to the college. I was a bit hesitant about contacting Hartley directly again. He had been on *Blue Peter* yesterday, telling of his experiences at Nasa. He looked different to how I remembered him, and he was wearing eyeliner.

I arranged to meet Shona 2 at the Griffin later. I was thinking about her a lot. She worked at the bank, but was desperate to become an actress. She had lost two stone and cropped her hair to play Peter Pan last Christmas, in a tour of three of the little village halls locally. She got a good review in one of the parish magazines, though she was slated in the local press for portraying too much of Peter's feminine side – not something the author ever intended apparently. It must be difficult having an artistic vision which no one understands.

Maria phoned while I was getting ready to go out. She wanted me to go round for a chat. She sounded quite desperate, but I said I had a headache and she didn't push. It wasn't that I didn't want to see her, I just wanted to see Shona more.

Shona was sitting at the bar. The pub was quieter these days. A lot of people had drifted to the White Horse after the accident, and the beer was 2p cheaper a pint. They only sold O'Malley's crisps though, which I thought was very short-sighted of them. Walker's are far fresher. Shona sat coyly sipping a mineral water, wearing a long dark skirt. She was about to play a nun in *The Sound of Music*. Unfortunately this meant experiencing chastity. When we first met she'd a small part in a new play about nymphomania. It was a cruel twist of fate.

We went to hear a band play at the Memorial Theatre: some group I hadn't heard of who had supported another group I hadn't heard of at Bournemouth six years ago. A friend on Shona's drama A level course had recommended them, but the music was too loud for the vocals and the singer sounded distant and muffled. Shona appeared to be enjoying herself. I found this irritating, because they really were shit. Maria would never have wanted to see a band like this, or expected me to pay for it. Fifteen quid each and I was broke, working nearly two weeks in hand. I thought maybe I'd give Maria a ring later when I got back. We could have a laugh about it.

★

It said on the news that Helstad had been bombed again, hundreds of families separated or killed. Mam was glued to the screen, desperate for some new development that would unite war-torn parents with their children. She wrote to the *Guardian* to voice her feelings on the subject. She took a long time to compose the letter, sitting on the sofa in the lounge with the pad on her lap, staring out of the window. She spent more time in the lounge than the kitchen these days; Tam was in there more. It took her over two hours to write the letter, and then she chucked it in the Aga and put the kettle on. It struck me that despite everything she must miss Da. There had been no word from him since we'd got back.

The house felt empty, five people to two was a big leap. I wandered round for a few hours and then decided to call on Shona 1. The sun was setting behind the disused factory as I walked towards the concrete silhouette. Shona was watching the news about the missing child. She came to the door blubbing, with an old blue teddy under her arm. I just wished she'd turn the bloody set off. I couldn't cope with this constant grief. I wondered if Mam would still be like Shona in a year's time.

An hour later I walked back down the piss-stained stairs and out on to the street. Shit. It was the first time I hadn't been able to perform. I could feel the cold sweat drying on my forehead. Fucking hell. Better not be the MacNab curse. That was all I needed.

As a nurse Mam had always been rather fanatical about hygiene. She would even make Da scrub up with surgical antiseptic before sex, according to Tam. As I let myself into the house that night it occurred to me that the place was a pigsty. There were jars left out in the kitchen, yesterday's dishes still soaking in the bowl, all the work surfaces covered in bits of pizza, empty carriers and crumbs from a burst loaf. There were no knives in the cutlery drawer when I went to make a sandwich and the bin was smeared with baked beans. Tomorrow, I thought to myself, maybe I'll clean up a bit. If I think of it. I retrieved Tam's walking boots from under the stairs. They were a good fit.

★

When I crawled home from work at six-thirty next morning, Cameron's coat was over the banister in the hall. He was back, then. Mam was delighted, though pissed off Da wasn't with him.

'What's he doing up there?' She rounded on Cameron as he ate a bowl of cornflakes.

'Having a holiday, first one he's had in years. You know he couldn't get away from the sheep before.'

'Oh well, in that case he should have axed them all to death years ago. Anyway what was Skegness if that wasn't a bloody holiday? Christ, our son's dead and he's having a sodding mid-season break.'

'*One* of your sons is dead.' I pointed out helpfully.

'So when's he coming back then? Because the hearing will be soon, and if they say he can't keep sheep he should be out there looking for a bloody job.'

'He'll be back for the hearing. You could have stayed up there with him.' Cameron chucked his bowl into the sink and wiped his mouth on his sleeve. Mam pursed her lips, turned the tap on and started to scrub the dishes, very hard.

*

The gypsies were back. Cameron and I watched them from the hillside, unloading their horses from a huge lorry. We sat on a bale of hay and looked at the pens. The grass had grown a good few inches, the ground looked less turfy. The sheep droppings scattered about had gone crusty and white in the sun. Some of the hurdles round the perimeter had fallen in, and a cow from next door was stretching its neck through for the cow parsley that was taking over. It was quite pleasant, really, sitting there in the sun, not talking much. The only reminder of what had happened were a few clumps of wool caught on thistles or wire. I picked a small clump that was near my foot and started teasing it out, the greasy grey fibres lengthening under the pull of my fingers, getting whiter as it grew longer. I threw it down in disgust when I found a dead tick in it, like a fat piece of sweetcorn. After a while we went home to tea.

By 6 p.m. I was hanging up my coat in the locker-room at work. It was horrible, knowing that I wasn't going to get any sleep, that while the rest of the world was winding down for the night, I was speeding up, my mind trying to override my body. It took me ten minutes to retrieve my card, which had jammed in the clocking-in machine.

'Other way up.' The charge-hand absent-mindedly scratched at a horsefly bite on his arm, distracted, I could tell, by the thought of gangrene and certain amputation. Twelve hours later I was on my way home again, with crippling backache from loading pallets, the sound of breaking glass ringing in my ears, carrying a box of beers which had had their labels stuck on upside-down.

★

I was at the local tech for an interview. I was a bit disappointed by the look of the place. There was one main building which ran in a square round a central courtyard. This bit had been used as a hospital in the last war. The whole corrugated roof lifted during storms. The rest of the site was made up of old wooden huts set side by side, with wooden steps and shabby doors. There was litter collected in the corner of the tarmacked walkway, and a torn map of the classrooms. I was here to find out about access courses for September. This was my route to university, I had finally concluded. I rubbed my eyes blearily. The head of further education, Mrs Palmer, was ten minutes late. She was an enormous woman with sweaty cheeks and a huge floral dress that was pegged to her shoes. If there had been a zip down the front I would have felt obliged to light a campfire and open some beans. She gave me an enthusiastic handshake. Handshakes are funny things in my opinion. They always catch you by surprise and then you kick yourself for not gripping the offered hand more firmly. We sat down and Jackie, as she asked me to call her, smiled widely and asked me to talk about what I wanted to do. A huge flood of things welled up in my mind, but when I opened my mouth nothing came out. Jackie spotted my indecision.

'Not sure? Well, why don't you tell me what your interests are?' Now was not the time to mention a fascination with S & M, I guessed.

'Astronomy,' I offered.

Jackie wrote this down. She wrote everything down in big round letters.

An hour later I was lighting a cigarette outside the college gates. It was settled: I was to take a general access course full-time for a year, and start deciding what university course interested me. The vague thought at the moment was that I'd apply for a teacher-training course for the eleven-to-sixteen age group, concentrating on science and technology, where the shortage was.

'You'll get a higher grant and much better chance of a job at the other end,' Jackie pointed out. I mused on this on the swings in the park with a Drumstick lolly and a packet of Fizzers.

Mam made me a packed lunch at lunchtime, to get me into the swing of going to college: a sweaty cheese slice in a frozen bap, and an economy orange juice drink. I took the lunchbox into the garden and made a fire out of the notes to my book. I watched the thin black lines that started at the edges and worked inwards, with the bright orange trim that led the way. After twenty minutes all that was left was a pile of ash strips, lit by the occasional spark. It was all over. I got the poker from the kitchen and stirred at the ashes, trying to burn the last few words that were still visible. A thousand sparks lifted and soared into the air, and a small flame struggled over the remaining bits of paper. I wiped my hands on my jeans and went inside. I realised later that I hadn't eaten my roll. The sweaty cheese slice had fallen on to the lawn and was being removed by ants.

That afternoon I helped Shona 2 move into her new flat. She had been sharing a house with six other students, but was sick of the endless piles of neon condoms and the absence of toilet paper. 'I bought twelve rolls last week – where have they gone?' Shona would be dead pleased I'd got a place at the tech. That was where she was taking her drama A level. I still hadn't got round to phoning Maria, who had left four or five messages for me at home.

The flat was all right, the landlord dead lucky to get a tenant like Shona. The previous one had left a candle burning in the bathroom and burnt the room down. The rest of the flat was saved by the plastic water pipes which melted in the heat and put the fire out. In the bedroom the tenant had even boarded up one of the windows with hardboard and kept the door shut for months, so when Shona viewed it there had been a foot of mould round the top of the walls. The place was pristine now though, and smelt of fresh paint, and only slightly of dogs.

It took us three hours to get all the boxes into the flat. Shona put the seats down in her Ford Fiesta and we could get four in at a time. The flat was small without being poky and Shona had been busy all week, painting and preening it. Plain walls were broken up by artily hung scarves and framed poems that I didn't understand but sounded good. It was arty, but all right really. It made me want my own place.

I was drinking tea with Maria in the kitchen. She had knocked and knocked at half past eight in the morning, so that she wouldn't miss me. I stumbled downstairs, conscious of the fact I had only been in bed for an hour. The day was sunny and mild I noticed as I opened the front door, a great day for walking in the country. I was in my Superman pyjamas but she didn't seem to notice. God, she looked different. I couldn't think what I'd ever seen in her. Her face was thin and as white as a piece of paper. Her hair was shorter, she kept tucking it behind her ear as she stared out of the window.

'Your da's garden's come on a treat. Ours is really overgrown at home, what with the baby – all the preparation I mean.' She gulped down a mouthful of tea.

'How's your work experience going?' was the best I could come out with.

'It's finished. I'm waiting now to start college. My grant will come through soon.'

As she spoke a huge tear plopped out of her eye like a contact lens. It was so heavy it missed her face and banged on to the table. She looked at me quickly and looked away again.

'Keith, I'm pregnant. What am I going to do?'

It took me a minute to remember that Tam was dead. And then to register the bit about the baby. No wonder she looked so bloody awful.

'Congratulations?' I offered.

It was the wrong thing to say. She looked at me incredulously and the single tear became a pile-up on the table.

Fuck.

'I can't tell Mum and Dad, because of their baby. I can't keep it, can I? I can't saddle myself with a baby now, can I? I'd have to give up college, never be able to make anything of my life. I don't want to spend the next five years shagging quietly so as not to wake a kid up, I can't do that, Keith, I don't want this.'

I bit a piece of muck out from under my thumbnail.

'Are you sure you're pregnant?'

Maria lifted up her jumper and showed me her belly. It looked a bit swollen. I'd never seen such an intimate part of Maria before. It was quite a turn-on actually.

'And it's not because you've been eating a lot?' The wrong thing to say.

Maria took her cup to the sink and tipped out the dregs. She's one of those people who never drink the last drop.

'I'm sorry, Keith.' I wished she wouldn't keep using my name. She picked up her bag and wiped a hand over her face. 'I shouldn't have come, it's not your problem.'

'What did you want me to do?'

She was right, it wasn't my problem. I was moving on.

'Pay for a termination, it would be four hundred quid private.'

There was no way. All my money was paying off Tam's debts. I couldn't afford to kill his baby as well.

'I can't. I haven't got it.'

'I thought you wouldn't, only it was best to ask. I'll see the doctor about NHS, I'll have to wait till it's three months – they make you, in case you miscarry first. It saves on a bed. It will have its fingers and toes. I read that in Mum's pregnancy magazine.'

'I really can't help.'

I washed out the cups, which was a first for me, and left them to drain on the side. Maria headed for the door and paused. 'Would you come with me when I go in? That would mean a lot to me.'

'S'pose so.' I hated hospitals When she left I had a quick look to check if anyone had seen her leave.

CHAPTER TWELVE

Shona looked over to me. We were lying in bed after the most incredible shag ever. It was our first time. Previously my sex life had consisted of a quick ten minutes and then a long walk home. This was something else, to fall asleep with someone, and to wake again, with furry teeth and a full bladder. It was the last night of *The Sound of Music*, and Shona's vow of chastity could be broken. I had sat through two hours of singing nuns in a room full of farting old ladies. Shona was the nun who sang about holding moonbeams in your hand. She was high with adrenalin all the way home, wondering whether she had been spotted by an agent. It was unlikely, I thought, in Horningsham Village Hall. It was annoying at first: as she took off her top and bra, all I could think about was Tam's baby. What would he have thought of it? He would have dumped Maria there and then. And I'd still have been left to sort it out. Anyway, it had been her choice. No one had forced her to go to bed with my brother rather than me.

Shona pulled me to her. She was mad for it, her nails scratching along my thighs. I leant forward and took her top lip between my teeth and bit down hard. She flinched instinctively and pushed her lower body against me. I pushed back and, like an anti-tug-of-war, we braced ourselves to remain upright, our bodies swaying against the pressure. And although she called out two other names when I was going full throttle, and I was thinking of Maria, it was still the shag of my life. Shona 2 beat Shona 1 hands down any day, though Shona 1 was dirtier, which was still an incredible turn-on, despite the fact she was quite old and wrinkly. This was what it was supposed to be like, I thought, as I looked back at Shona's flushed face: sex between two people attracted to each other, rather than just sex for its own sake.

★

There was a huge suitcase on Mam's bed, several full bin liners on the floor. Mam was sitting on the floor looking at things us kids had made her when we were little – Mother's Day cards with squashed paper daffodils, Christmas decorations made from egg-boxes coated in glitter, that sort of crap.

'Look at this, Keith.' She held out a picture of a car, a crayony scribble. 'That was the first thing Tam did at school. He brought it home on his first day.'

'Oh, right.'

'I hope your da will be back before I leave. He has to be back soon. I'm leaving on Tuesday.'

'Have you spoken to him?' I sat on the bed and stared out of the window. In the garden a cat was peeing in Da's flowerbed.

'Not a word since Scotland. Do you think he's all right?' She looked at me for reassurance.

'He's not on his own, is he? If you're worried you could always ring him at Doug's.' The cat was scraping at the earth now, digging it back to reveal the white head of a daffodil bulb.

Mam set her face. 'No, he's the one that's gone AWOL. He knows how to contact me.' She screwed up the picture in her hand and chucked it in the bin liner.

★

It was nearly the end of summer. The woods were looking parched now; even the muddiest tracks had dried out into ruts that made your legs ache. The shooting was nearly over for the year. There would be the cull of the male pheasants, then the white barriers would be unlocked and in would come the local horses, turning the ground to mud again as soon as it rained. Mam would be gone by the time my college course started. Da had to be back soon.

Maria was waiting for me when I got home. She had a date for the abortion. We went up to my room and I sat on the bed as she stared out of the window.

'Is it true your da killed the sheep?'

'Yeah.'

'Why'd he do it?'

'Dunno.'

She was quiet for a few minutes. 'Will you take me to the hospital?'

'Yeah.'

'Cheers.' She seemed to take for ever walking down the two flights of stairs to the front door, as if she didn't really want to leave. I was anxious; I was due at Shona's. In the end I bounded past her and had the door open all ready for her. She bit her lip as she walked out.

Shona cooked me a meal that night. It was a disgusting slop of kidney beans and a runny sauce. I'd never liked kidney

159

beans – too much like eating beetles. We ate at a low coffee table sitting on the floor facing the telly. Afterwards I helped her learn her lines for her new part, as Antigone in the Frome Player's autumn production.

'If we can go from the top, down to page fifty, I'll do the rest at work tomorrow.' Shona worked full-time for Barclays. She spent a lot of her working day making origami frogs that jumped. The rest she spent learning lines.

★

We sat in bed watching the late film and eating chocolates. It felt strange, sleeping in bed at night, rather than against wooden pallets, without the dust-cart to wake me up, or the milk-float. The factory was cutting back on agency staff, or so they said. Maybe I wasn't fast enough: I used to let bottles smash rather than boxing them, because sweeping involved more physical exercise. The charge-hand had called me into his office, handed me a round ball of mature chedder and delivered a thanks-but-no-thanks speech.

'When your mam goes away, why don't you move in here?' Shona bit into a soft centre.

'I couldn't afford to, not with Tam's debts to clear. I couldn't afford rent as well.'

'You know legally you're not entitled to pay that money. It was Tam's debt, which should be taken out of his estate. If there's no money, there's no money. Anyway, surely your parents could clear the amount? It's only a couple of grand.'

She obviously did more at work than she let on, and her parents were clearly in a different financial league altogether.

'Which jumping frog told you that then? If I stop paying, the letters will start coming and Da will find out about Tam. I'm doing this for Mam.' That was a lie. I was doing this 'cause I couldn't face the hassle, the thought of Mam going on and on about it.

'Maybe your da would think more of you if he knew about this.' Shona closed the lid on the chocolates. She was trying to put on weight. She wanted her Antigone to be quite fleshy, as a stand against male ideals or something.

'Haven't you got anything you can sell to clear the debt?' We both knew that she was referring to the telescope.

'Leave it out. It would be like selling an arm or a leg.'

★

I got three and a half grand for it. The first person who saw it snapped it up straightaway. 'Bloody bargain, mate, these buggers are difficult to find.' The man was slavering. Too bloody right. I'd never be able to afford another one. I watched the man bundle it into his van, clutching seventy cheques for fifty quid in my dry hand. I winced as he caught the lens on the door.

I went for a long walk. There was a lot I had to get straight in my head. The fact that I couldn't go backwards hit me hard. I wasn't a kid. Moving out signalled this, more than having sex or selling a prize possession. The burden of maturity clawed at me, raking up a massive hole in the bottom of my stomach, and an overwhelming sense of loss hit into my bowel. There was a squashed pheasant fluttering in the road as I crossed the bypass. Flies were eating into a cut on its belly. Both its legs were dangling. I took its neck in my hands and, using its weight, throttled it. I felt better after that. I chucked it into the ditch and crossed the road.

★

Mam was concerned when I said I was moving out.

'What about Da? He'll need your support, I hoped me going away would bring you two closer together.'

'It's just down the road. It's high time I moved out.' It was with a heavy wallet that I cleared Tam's credit-card bill. Two and a half thousand in total, what with the interest, the bank charges, and the bank staff's Christmas bonus. A new life. A new career. A new home. Financial freedom. Keith MacNab begins here.

★

Da was sitting in the kitchen drinking tea.

'Does Mam know you're back?' I couldn't believe he looked so different: with six weeks growth of beard and a tam-o'-shanter stuck to his head.

'Course she fucking knows. She's gone down the shops to get some food.' He was tearing a page of newspaper into shreds, his hands looked chafed and sore.

'You all right?' I queried, bravely.

'Make us some more tea will you? Pot's gone cold.' He stuffed a wad of paper in his mouth and started to chew.

'Have you seen Cameron?' I filled the kettle and lifted the lid off the hot plate.

'No, not since Scotland. He should never have come back. Doug would have let him stay on. He should never have come back.'

I left Da chewing at the table.

We had one of our famous family meals that night. Mam cooked an enormous shepherd's pie and we all tucked in. The conversation was strained, to say the least. Half-way through the meal Da's fork clattered on to the stone floor and he stooped to pick it up. His head came up so sharply that he banged it on the table. I struggled not to laugh. 'What you got on your feet, Keith?'

I lost the desire to laugh.

'What you doing wearing Tam's boots? Who said he could wear them? Did you tell him, Rosemary?'

Mam looked at us both blankly. Da's fist came out and caught me on the jaw. I shot backwards nearly coming off my chair. It fucking hurt.

'Take them off, you hear me?'

'For God's sake, Michael, does it matter? Tam's hardly going to need them is he?'

'Take them off.'

Da bent down and grabbed my foot and tried to pull the laced boots clean off.

'Get off him, Michael, this isn't helping.'

'Get the fucking thing off.'

A shower of cutlery and condiments hit the floor. Da tugged. I thought my foot was coming off as well. He was twisting and pulling; he was going to break my ankle. I felt the swelling rise on my face. I caught Da straight in his eye. I wasn't sure where I was aiming. I just knew it had to be hard enough to get him to stop. He stopped. He dropped my ankle and cried out, cradling his eye. There was blood on my knuckles and I started to panic. Christ, what had I done? I got up and ran out before Da could retaliate. I was six again, or eight or ten. As I ran I heard Da's voice.

'Bloody useless. He was too close. He ruined the momentum.'

'He still hit you, though.' Mam dabbed at his eye with a napkin.

*

I didn't stop running till I was well past Keyford and heading down towards the bypass. The traffic was heavy, the smell of petrol fumes hitting the bottom of my lungs and threatening to plaster the tarmac with the undigested contents of my stomach. I slowed to a steady jog, realising that I was attracting too much attention, and kept up the pace for several miles, my breathing coordinating with my legs, the burning in my calves subsiding as my warm muscles stretched with the movement. Eventually I doubled over, my head between my knees. Tam's boots were still firmly tied to my feet. The blood on my knuckles had dried and was flaking off, leaving a faint brown smudge. I couldn't get that look of surprise on Da's face out of my head. My watch said it was eight o'clock.

It was after eleven when I got home. I kicked the boots under the stairs. I could smell my socks as I slipped quietly up to bed.

★

We were in the waiting room of the Victoria Cross hospital. Maria had an appointment with the consultant, to talk over what would happen during the termination. The room was a depressing grey, with pictures of smiling faces stuck on the wall. There was a fish tank in the corner with two dead fish bobbing on the top of the filthiest water imaginable. A pink plastic castle was on its side at the bottom of the tank.

'I hope the operating theatre is more hygienic.'

Maria didn't answer. She was staring at the cover of *Mother and Baby* on the seat next to her.

The consultant looked as if he had been on duty all night. He smelt of coffee and surgical scrub.

'Right, you're the one for the termination are you?'

'And you're the father. Anyone ever told you to tie a knot in it?' He peered at my muddy trainers.

'There was a mat for wiping your shoes at the entrance you know.'

From then on he ignored me.

'A termination is not a substitute for contraception, you know. I'm not some kind of morning-after pill. We are short of beds. Someone waiting for an operation will have to wait longer because of you.' He frowned over the top of his National Health specs. 'Can I ask which method of contraception it is that you are having problems with?'

Maria was looking distressed, clutching at her chair. 'I'm only doing this because the father was killed.'

'Well who's this then, the resurrection?' The consultant pointed at me with his pen.

★

The war in Albania was over. It was official. The prime minister had resigned and the government had been overturned. On the news each night for the last two years we had been shown pictures of the latest bombing victims, rows of hospital beds full of people with severed limbs and bandaged heads. Mam was straight on the phone to the agency.

'Where does this leave me? I'm all set to go.' She tapped on the table with her Biro. 'Well, that's a relief.' She put the receiver down and went back to shelling peas. 'They'll still need nurses for several months yet, and after that they will move me on.'

'Perhaps they'll start fighting again, just so that you get to keep your job.' The irony was lost.

★

Maria was ready when I drove up in Da's Granada. Mrs Alder waved out of the window. 'Have a lovely time, darling. See you tomorrow.'

'She thinks we're staying the night in the New Forest,' Maria informed me as she buckled her seat-belt.

The car park was full. We drove round and round and in the end Maria jumped out and went on in. By the time I found her she had been installed in a bed covered in paper sheets. She was wearing her nightie and a male doctor had stuck a stethoscope down her front. Baby's other end, I thought, as he had a good rummage. There was a pile of magazines on the little bedside table, all containing pictures of babies.

'Right, well, I'll see you later,' I said when the doctor had gone.

'Yeah, thanks for bringing me.' She gave me a look as if to say, Please don't go, but I was meeting Shona at eleven. We were going shopping at Sainsbury's together – a sort of trial for when I moved in.

'You'll be fine.'

She blinked and nodded. I stopped and smoked a cigarette outside the front doors of the hospital.

Sainsbury's was a success. We took it in turn to sit in the trolley and bought sensible things like toilet rolls, as well as goodies. Shona's parents never bought toilet rolls from the market: they were very middle-class and preferred softer paper. We went back to Shona's and crashed out for the afternoon, watching videos and drinking beer. It wasn't until half-past four that I remembered I had to phone the hospital. Shit. I said goodbye to Shona and let myself out of the flat.

A load of junkies were injecting themselves with Persil on

the corner of Coffin Street, slapping each other's veins and then shooting up on a warm rinse. The road was full of empty syringes and soap suds. I stopped at a callbox and phoned the number Maria had given me. The nurse who answered said Maria was waiting to be picked up.

'But I thought she was staying in overnight?'

'With our waiting lists, I don't think so. Ward Three is a day ward.'

I was too pissed to drive properly. It took me ten minutes to realise that I hadn't turned the key in the ignition. I drove slowly, kicking myself for being so stupid.

When I arrived Maria was standing in a pool of blood by the bed. An Irish nurse was telling her off for getting up.

'I was desperate for a pee.' Maria sat on the bed. She was still in her nightie, a red stain turning to brown as the blood soaked into the material.

'Keith!' She didn't seem to realise I was late, she was so friggin' pleased to see me.

She held my hand awkwardly while the nurse looked away, as if I was somehow responsible.

Another nurse came up with a giant pad of cotton wool and told Maria to put it in her knickers.

'I'll be in the waiting area.' I backed off, knocking a vase of flowers off a table. 'Sorry about that.'

The nurse muttered something under her breath.

After ten minutes Maria came out, walking very slowly. It couldn't be comfortable walking with a thing like that stuffed in her pants.

'God, Keith, I'm desperate for a pee.' She looked round for the toilets.

'There were some by the entrance.'

Her face was like a carrier bag, dead white with freckles standing out like a shop logo. I waited twenty minutes in the hall while she went for a piss. She eventually came out in tears.

'I can't fucking do one, it must be the anaesthetic.'

I was careful not to drive over any bumps on the way home. Maria made me stop at the Spar so that she could buy a box of fudge and a postcard of an Exmoor pony.

'She'll never notice it's not a New Forest one.' Maria winced as she sat back down in the car. 'Can I stay over at your place tonight? I can't face going home. Mum will wonder why I came back early.'

I couldn't say no. I hoped to God Shona didn't try to come round.

We ate fish and chips in my bedroom. They blotted out the smell of surgical scrub. The windows were tightly shut to keep the moths out.

'Thank God that's over with.' Maria was picking at her food. 'The anaesthetist kept talking about rabbits. Then the bastard stuck a needle in the back of my hand.'

Mam and Da were arguing downstairs. Lines like 'We never were a proper family, or this thing with Tam would have brought us closer together' were drifting upstairs.

'I'm sorry, Keith, you've got your own problems. When's your Mam leaving?'

'The day after tomorrow.'

'I'll come to the airport if you want, to see her off.' Maria and mam had always got on all right.

'Erm . . . See how you are, you might not be up to it.' She still hadn't managed to have a pee. Besides, Shona had said she'd come. It was getting awkward.

*

Maria took my bed and I slept on the floor. A few months ago the thought of Maria in my bed would have blown my mind. Now I just hoped she wouldn't get blood on the sheet.

★

The next morning I woke to the sound of someone having an enormous piss. It went on and on and I fell back to sleep dreaming of the Indian monsoon.

'Keith, can I have a cuddle?' Maria shook me awake. Her hair was frizzed up round her face. She crept under my blanket and I put my arm round her. 'It's weird, us here together like this.'

Too right it was weird. If Shona could see me now.

'I lied before, to the police, about not remembering anything when we crashed. I just couldn't say.'

'Say what?'

'I told him that I liked you.'

I froze. I wished she wouldn't keep saying this. It was too fucking late. I didn't want to hear it. 'You were going out with him.'

'Because you didn't want to know. I figured that it was better to go out with your brother than no one. Christ, if you'd given me any indication at all that you fancied me, I would never have gone near him.'

'So how did the crash happen?' It seemed macabre asking that, like I was peeping in on someone undressing, something private.

'I told him it was over. I couldn't handle seeing you all the time. He was out of his head anyway and he drove like a bloody maniac, and – Christ – I saw the wall coming. It was fucking awful. I've killed your brother and his baby, yet I can't keep away from you.'

Then we had sex. With Maria sobbing into my mouth. It wasn't how I'd ever imagined it would be. Her stomach hurt too much for me to go on top so she sat on me, pushing and writhing on to me as if she had a huge internal itch that she wanted to scratch. With her tears plopping on to my face as she pushed herself down on me. I knew that this was the best ever shag I had ever had, would ever have. It was like we were colouring a picture in, the empty spaces slowly being filled.

We lay side by side in silence. Suddenly Maria sat up and exclaimed, 'Where's your telescope gone?' Her tits were swollen from being pregnant.

'I sold it.'

'Why?'

'I needed the money.'

'It meant so much to you! God I was so jealous of it. All the times I wanted to be with you and you wanted to look at the fucking sky. I felt so bloody inadequate.'

I noticed that there was blood on me. And on the sheet. It suddenly struck me, 'You can't get pregnant again, can you?'

CHAPTER THIRTEEN

We were at the airport, me, Mam, Shona and Cameron. Mam wasn't pleased that Shona was there, as she couldn't go all mumsy on us. The airport was packed with screaming kids and pissed-off parents. Mam was wearing an awful suit that she had bought from Oxfam so that she wouldn't look too overdressed to the officials who were to meet her at the other end.

'I want them to take me seriously. I don't want to look like a tourist,' she had said as I helped her do the zip up on the skirt. Da had been in the kitchen, reading the *Mail*, flicking ash from his cigarette into a saucer. He had been there all morning, moving only to put a shovelful of coal into the Aga.

'Your father should have been here.' Mam was in a flap, dropping her ticket and then her passport.

'Why would Da be here? I wish I wasn't here.' Cameron pursed his lips and studied the departures board overhead.

'You're big enough to look after yourself. Some men are married with children at your age: your da was.' Mam dropped her ticket again.

'Anyway, the weather will be good out there. You'll be ever so brown.' Shona's fantasy was a bronzed Antigone, and she made regular trips to a sunbed to achieve this aim.

'Albania is in Europe. You're probably thinking of Tanzania or something.' Mam was unnecessarily sharp. 'I don't think a suntan will be at the top of my list of priorities anyway.'

Shona wandered off to look round the souvenir shops.

'For God's sake, Keith, fancy taking up with a girl like that. She hasn't got an ounce of sense in her entire body.' Mam wasn't being fair.

'She really wanted to come and see you off.'

'Well, didn't you think I'd rather spend time with you and Cameron?'

They were calling her flight number, asking all passengers to board. Mam was ignoring it, looking angrily at me, before she gave me a hug.

'Maria is such a lovely girl, you could really make it happen with her. I know she stayed with you last night. It was always right for you two, except you were both too stupid to realise it.' She let me go.

'Are you going to catch this bloody plane or not, Mam?' Cameron was bored, picking at his nails.

Mam hugged Cameron and then me again.

'I love you two, and I'll be back at Christmas for a holiday. I'll call you as soon as I can.'

We watched her get smaller as she disappeared into the crowd. We stood there for a while, before Shona rejoined us, clutching several carriers.

'Have I missed her? Oh well, that's done now. Let's find a pub,' she said as if we had just taken the dog for a walk.

Da was still sitting at the kitchen table when we got home. Cameron sat down next to him and I followed suit quite nervously. I hadn't talked to him since he went ballistic over the walking boots.

'And then there were three, eh?' Da laughed without any humour.

'We'll work something out, Da, yeah?' Cameron briefly touched Da's arm.

There were no suitcases left: Mam had taken them all. I started stuffing clothes into Spar bags. Shona wanted me to move in straight away, and I knew that if I stayed I'd have got stuck with Da's problems. The end of his world was the start of my new one. I had a girlfriend, a flat, a career lining up. Mam had gone. I was eighteen, an adult. Today is the first day of the rest of my life, I told myself, not for the first time, as I stuffed balls of socks into a plastic bag. In a way sleeping with Maria had exorcised Tam. It was like everything had happened in the wrong order. I should have slept with Maria before Tam did, and it was as if someone had taken my life cards and thrown them up in the air. I was stuck with where they landed. I didn't know what to say to Maria when I saw her.

Cameron and Da had gone to the pub when I took my things down to the hall. I left a note explaining where I was going, and a cheque for a grand. That left me with five hundred quid. I didn't expect him to keep the money, I expected him to come round and force it down my throat. As it was he did keep it, I tried not to mind.

We were at a club. Shona wanted us to celebrate my moving in. It was good, feeling this free. As the music pumped into my veins I felt the knots in my stomach relax. Shona was dancing manically, out of it on E or something. I spent a lot of time at the bar, downing beer after beer.

'Come and dance.' Shona loomed at me. Her pupils the size of saucers.

'In a minute. This song's crap.'

'No, now.' She grabbed at my hand and missed. She tried again and I helped her by holding my hand out very still. 'Stop waving it about, will you, and dance.'

I stumbled after her. The drink had gone straight to my head, but it didn't matter. Nothing fucking mattered except the beat, the lights, and the screw I was going to have when I got home.

At three o'clock we went outside and waited for a taxi to pull up. We were giggling as we stuck our tongues down each other's throats. Unfortunately Shona's went down a little too far and I started retching. And then so did she. We each produced a pile of sick in the alleyway, and then we cracked up, almost wetting ourselves. When a taxi came at last we were knackered and dozed on each other's shoulders, taking it in turns to put our heads on top. We woke up suddenly as the taxi driver swore and swerved. Orange flames were shooting through the windows of my old school. We could see the grey of the smoke fogging the sky.

'Bloody hell, must be dodgy wiring,' the taxi driver commented.

I friggin' hoped so. When we pulled up outside the flat, the taxi driver grinned and tapped his meter.

'That'll be forty quid, then, son.'

'Forty quid? It's only half a mile up the road.'

'Ah, but I've been driving round for two hours waiting for you to wake up.' Bloody bastard. I didn't tip him.

★

We woke the next morning to the sound of a lorry reversing up the road. Shona's flat was in a converted mill cottage. It

174

was funny being somewhere without a view. The bedroom looked out on to a carpark which was full of small children after school, racing round on bikes or sitting picking at the tarmac.

'Do you want some breakfast?' Shona yawned. She looked a sight first thing in the morning. Her eyes were pinheads after last night's excesses.

Shona was a bit of a tidiness freak. I hadn't realised this before last night. She made me fold my clothes neatly and put them on a chair. And she made me spend twenty minutes clearing up a pile of vomit that had missed the toilet, rinsing the stain with hot then cold water and then applying nearly a whole bottle of Vanish. 'Sick stains so much. Something to do with the stomach acid I guess.'

Mam usually cleared the vomit at home. It was just one of those things she did. It was all part of being self-reliant this cleaning-up crap.

Shona brought me breakfast in bed, like I was a kid off school.

'Please don't get crumbs in bed. I'll have to change all the sheets.' She kissed the top of my head and checked her hair in the mirror – 'I'll be back about six. Could you make a start on dinner.' – and then she was off, to spend a day making jumping frogs at Barclays.

I wandered round the flat for a bit. This was the first time I'd been here on my own. I looked in the fridge and in all the cupboards. Shona had already unpacked my clothes and put them in the chest of drawers we were sharing. Some of my T-shirts she put straight in the bin. I found a box of photographs in a cupboard in the kitchen, of Shona when she was at school, with her mates and several blokes. One bloke appeared frequently in the pictures. It was weird, seeing photos of someone Shona had known first, weird seeing someone's lives in pictures, a freeze-framed history that made me feel left out. I was at a loose end, in someone else's home. Normally at this time I would watch the kid's programmes with a box of cereal, but it didn't feel right here. It was obviously going to take a bit of getting used to. You couldn't just take one life and put it in another place without it feeling any different. I felt a sharp stab of homesickness for a warm, wet bed and the comforting smell of urine on my arms, the smell that would linger all day at school and tide me over till I got home again.

★

We went to Brean Sands at the weekend. We drove on to the beach and along to the cliffs, where we parked up. The tide was a thin line of blue in the distance. Shona opened the car door. There was a scream and the door slammed again. I got out. It was like someone had chucked a bucket of sand in my face. I couldn't see and could feel the grit under my eyelids.

'It's a bit breezy.' Shona rubbed her eyes. She was covered in a fine layer of yellow, like a golden retriever.

We put our towels on the beach and sheltered, half under the car. Nearby a child licked at an ice cream that was covered in sand. Everyone else was wearing sunglasses to protect themselves. Shona rolled over and looked at me.

'Do you think we'll fall in love?'

It was a funny question, her lying there with the exhaust of the car just above her head. It wasn't something that I had thought of; it seemed too early for that. I didn't feel capable of loving anyone, unless love was the urge to have sex with someone more than once, but then that meant I loved Shona 1, which I didn't. I thought of Maria, what I felt about her. The ache that I got when she was going out with Tam, the feelings I had that night after the abortion, the burning, pulsing ache I felt when we kissed.

'Dunno, 'spect so.' I took a peach out of the picnic basket and bit deep.

Shona exclaimed, 'Oh, Keith, you've got juice on the towel.'

We lay in silence for a while, watching the children run along the shore. The cliffs were above us, a vertical carpet of yellow flowers.

'Let's get an ice cream.' We braved it along the beach, with our eyes shut and the sand stinging our legs. A red flag warned about the danger of swimming, which was funny, because you couldn't see the sea at all now. Perhaps the exertion of walking out that far could be dangerous. We sat outside the little café eating our cones, the wind making it difficult to use my tongue efficiently, the wafer going mushy in my fingers. On the next table a tray of tea blew off and smashed on the floor, covering everyone with drops of burning water. I didn't remember this from when we were little. I must have blanked it.

We had a shower together that evening. I lathered the soap and smeared bubbles over Shona's body. She looked beautiful, shiny and sleek. I rubbed soap into her nipples till they stood out hard in the palms of my hands. Maybe this could be love, I thought as I pushed myself into her, her leg wrapped over the side of the bath. I wasn't sure if sex was love, or if it really mattered anyway.

★

Shona's face was touching mine when I woke next morning, her cheek against my nose. With horror I realised she was covered in blood. My hand went instinctively to my nose, which was sticky. There were tell-tale smears on the pillow. Shit. I pulled the pillowcase off and used it to wipe my nose before I chucked it in the washing machine. I wasn't sure what to do about Shona, sleeping peacefully with the contents of my burst blood vessel plastered across her face. I dampened a flannel and very carefully scrubbed at her cheek and her eyebrows. There was even blood on her top lip. She sighed and turned over, 'Stuart, get off.'

She was clean now, her face looked strangely empty with her eyes closed. She didn't look dead, like Tam had done. His face had reminded me of a rubber mask human but with the contents wiped out, the bits that made him a person gone. Shona looked more like a television on standby, one flick of a button and she was back. Her eyes opened on cue.

'Oh, Keith, you don't use flannels do you, they are so unhygienic.'

★

There was a report on the news about the state of the hospitals in Albania. They showed footage of crammed wards, people sleeping on floors and rows of empty medicine cupboards. One nurse was holding up a newborn baby whose mother was dying of pneumonia.

'What hope is there?' the nurse was saying to a translator, who was trying to light a cigarette. I was hoping to see Mam in the background. I didn't know what hospital she would be at. There was a woman with dark hair in the distance, pushing an old man in a wheelchair, but I thought it probably wasn't her. She was too short.

In the post was a flat-warming card from Auntie Sage. I had always wished that Sage were my mother. Sage was fun when we were kids, like the time when she took us midnight swimming. The sky was black the moon hidden behind clouds that had been torn into strips. We all walked, whispering quietly with excitement, over the stones, yelping when a sharp edge cut home. The tide was high, moving like a thick duvet, heavy with seaweed, the smell of sewage wafting out into the night. I stuck out my tongue and licked the salt from the air.

'We're lucky it's a clear night.' Sage was wearing a green swimming costume. 'See that star system? That's the Great Bear.' I looked up, expecting to see an animal, but seeing fairy lights on a Christmas tree, dense with needles. I stood transfixed, conscious of splashing coming from all round me. A wave lapped at my feet, snapping me back to reality. Three dark shapes were in front of me, slowly vanishing into the water until I could only see heads, bobbing like seals. I sank to my knees and felt the water rise over my shoulders. I gasped and went under. One, two, three. Then I stood up, feeling the cold and the salt stinging my skin, the adrenalin smacking through my body. I shivered and dug my toes into the tiny pebbles and sand. The water was too cold for me. I climbed up the shingle bank, the taste of salt numbing my lips, and watched the others larking about, splashing and ducking each other. From the bungalow I could hear Mam and Da shouting, their voices magnified in the night. I put my hands over my ears and shut them out, counting the little beads of light that sparkled on to the moving tide.

'She's your family, I never said I wanted to come.'

I stuck the card up on my pinboard and decided to go to Sainsbury's.

Sainsbury's was nearly empty at lunchtime. It took me ages to find the tinned peaches. As I did I stepped back and bumped into a trolley. It was Maria's.

'Keith, hi! I've been ringing but no one's been answering.'

You would never guess she'd had an abortion a week ago. She looked great, like she used to. I felt a rush of adrenalin whiz up me, like bubbles in a Coke bottle. She was in a pair of tight jeans and her stomach looked flat. Her face was comfortingly familiar, like looking in the mirror. 'I've been out a lot.'

We were in the way, people waiting behind both of us, but we didn't move. 'Do you want to do something after here, go for a walk?' Maria held my gaze, her eyes very readable. I ought to say no.

'Yeah, all right, if you're up to it.' I couldn't drag my eyes from her. It shocked me how much it affected me, seeing her like this. A tremendous ache was building up through every part of me, not just my groin.

We loaded our carriers into her car. We drove to the Horse and Groom, then walked all the way up the mile-long gallop to Heaven's Gate. We sat side by side and studied Longleat House in the distance. We chatted for two hours, continuing conversations we'd had before Tam. She was vivid and funny, and I found myself looking at her for longer than I should. 'It's really autumny isn't it? I'm going to miss this.'

I was thinking of different scenarios. I was confused. I knew I shouldn't be here, but wanted to be. I knew my feelings for Maria were more than I could admit to myself.

'Why?'

'I'm off to university next week. I want to get settled in to the halls of residence before the term starts. They've given me a book list as long as your arm to read beforehand. Had you forgotten I was going?'

'No, not really.'

The decision was taken out of my hands. It was a relief.

*

It was past six o'clock when Maria dropped me off. I still hadn't told her that I'd moved; I got her to drop me off at the end of the road. I didn't want to bump into Cameron or Da yet. It took me ten minutes to hike across town. I stopped at the Indian for a takeaway. Shona was watching the news as I came crashing through the door at a hundred miles per hour.

'I'm sorry, got held up in Sainsbury's and then the Indian was busy.'

Shona was tired from eight hours of origami. She unpacked the Sainsbury's bags as I dished up the curry.

'These weren't on the list, were they?' Shona held out a pack of super-absorbent sanitary towels. I blinked. She also pulled out a kohl eyeliner and a copy of *Pregnancy Now* magazine. 'Keith, it's way too early to be thinking about a family. I've got my career to think of.'

I kept quiet. I was thinking fast.

'You must have picked up someone else's bags at the checkout.' She pulled out a bag of guinea-pig food and some cheap-looking toilet rolls. 'You'd never have bought those.'

'That's right, I must have done.' My brain was working overtime wondering what Maria was going to find in my carrier.

'Oh well, I can use these.' Shona popped the sanitary towels into a cupboard. 'They're incredibly thick though, like you'd use after having a baby or something.'

I tipped pilau rice on to a plate. Easy, nice and relaxed, I told myself.

★

The agency phoned to say they had more work for me. Shona gave me her car keys and I drove to Smarts at Warminster. Shona had been nagging me to get my own car. Da's was out of bounds now and Shona was a bit precious about hers. I said I'd look into it.

'Doesn't have to be anything flash, just an old banger.' I didn't know if I wanted one. I couldn't get it out of my head the day Tam and Cameron had come home with the Ford Escort, how excited they were.

'I will,' I said to Shona. 'Something low-key.'

It turned out my job consisted of shovelling prawns with a spade into a large bucket. I then mixed in some mayonnaise to make prawn cocktails. I had to wear a blue hairnet and a hat like they do in chip shops. It was compulsory to shave before each shift or you would be required to wear a beard net. If anything this job was worse than all the others, the stench of seafood nauseating. I got a rash from wearing rubber gloves that were too tight. The pay was appalling. My first pay packet only just cleared my share of the rent. It was galling, working for forty hours and being worse off than on the dole. The prawns were mainly from Iceland, and needed to be thawed before cooking. I relieved my boredom by slipping in the occasional eye on a stalk, or octopus beak that had escaped quality control. The building was ultra-modern, lit by huge strip lights that hung from the ceiling, making everything look slightly blue. When it was quiet I would hold a block of ice with a prawn inside up to the light, and study it in its immobility, freeze-framed, like a member of royalty in its glass coffin. Then I would pop it in my mouth, suck it till it thawed and then enjoy the slightly crunchy consistency. It's incredible how hungry you get in the middle of the night.

★

I was at the garage a few days later, checking what was available at what price. It was quiet for a Saturday. The streets were almost empty; Must be a match on, I thought to myself as I passed the market, where traders were offering their wares to invisible customers.

'Hello, Keith.'

I jumped. Da was standing right behind me. He was a bit too close and I felt awkward. I had never noticed before that his nose was shaped like a parrots beak. I could see the pores, large and open, with the occasional dark hair protruding. There was a strong smell of onions. 'Da, all right?' My hand instinctively started screwing up the wad of notes I was holding deep in my palm.

'I haven't seen you about.'

I nodded, trying to look natural.

'Whilst I'm here, I just wanted to say that money came in useful.'

'Oh, right,' Damn, no chance of a thousand-pound top-up for the car then.

'Cheers for the shopping as well, Maria dropped it in.'

'Oh, right.' I don't know why, but when I'm nervous I repeat the same line over and over.

'You could always come over for your tea sometime.' Da still hadn't shaved. His beard was getting very bushy. He looked like a kid who had dressed itself for the first time.

'Oh, right, cheers. I mean, I will.'

He was still close, looming at me with circles of red round his eyes. I wanted to step back without being obvious.

'Could do with the company to tell the truth. Cameron just mopes around like a wet weekend, it does my head in.'

'Oh, right.'

'And what with this court case coming up. I've got a date now, next week.'

'Oh, right.'

'Anyway, I'll let you go. Looking for a car are you?'

'Just a set of wheels to get me to work really.'

'You're doing all right for yourself son, I'm proud of you.' The words came out in such a whisper I nearly missed them.

★

It was on the news that there was no life on Mars. The ultrasound device the Americans had launched into space had misinterpreted radiation changes. Woolworths immediately withdrew their toy aliens from display. No one was surprised: people had stopped walking along with their noses in the sky months ago. How did we know it wasn't all lies anyway, that we hadn't been fed a load of crap to detract from the American and British bombings on Albania? Was it a coincidence that as soon as the war was over, so were the space reports? Anyway, it was of no interest to me any more. I wondered how my telescope was getting on. I hoped the man was being careful with the lens because they cost a fortune to replace.

Shona and I drove down to Stonehenge. It occurred to me that it was still Shona and I rather than we. I got home from work at 6.30 a.m. The mornings were dark now, a distant red haze to the east instead of the low yellow ball that made me blink and swerve. The drive home was always difficult, the momentum of the tyres lulling me to sleep. Occasionally I would turn over and snuggle into the seat, until the beep of an oncoming vehicle would make my knee jerk and I would grasp the wheel, vaguely wondering why the landing light hadn't been left on.

The carpark was silent as I pulled in behind the wheelie bins and stretched, my muscles aching from eight hours' work.

I vaguely remembering staggering to the front door and up the stairs to the top floor. I put the key in the lock and before the door could even swing open there was Shona, bright and fresh and horribly awake.

'Morning. Could you put this in the car? I'll just grab my bag and then we will be off.'

I turned obediently on my heel and staggered back down the stairs and out of the main door. The distant red haze was turning orange now. Women's handbags never fail to amaze me, I thought to myself, as Shona came up behind me clutching black leather. How can one small area carry so much junk and crap? Mam's was the same, only bigger. I suppose the older you are the more junk you need to carry around with you. I thought of Auntie Fran's little pull-along trolley and concluded I must be right: it gets so big it has to be put on wheels.

Shona drove while I slept deeply, crashed out on the back seat with my feet out of the window.

When I woke my thumb was in my mouth, the seat cover dark with dribble. The red haze had now vanished behind clouds and there was a constant drumming of rain on the roof. 'This is typical. Just when we need to spend more time together.' Shona unwrapped a Starburst and put the wrapper in the glove compartment.

Her comments surprised me. I had thought it was just me who had this constant ache for something more, this fear of missing out, the terror of settling for anything rather than nothing. I looked at her in the mirror as I climbed into the front. Shona instinctively brushed an invisible speck of mud from under the gear stick, though I knew my boots were clean. 'You really stink of prawns.' I couldn't do anything right, so I switched the radio on. 'Can you turn it down? My bloody head's throbbing.'

When we arrived at Stonehenge it was closed. Two security guards were walking up and down the perimeter fence. We parked on the side of the road and got out, standing in the pouring rain. I watched the drops settle on Shona's chest; I could see two hard bumps through the material. Shona crossed her arms defensively and got back into the car. I lit a cigarette, to annoy more than anything, and lent against the bonnet. Shona started the engine and it throbbed against me.

When we got back there was a car for sale in the flat's car-park, an old Renault 5 with stained upholstery and red speckles of rust protruding through the paintwork. It was two hundred and fifty pounds according to the cardboard sign taped to the inside of the windscreen.

'Just the job for your missus.' The owner was there in a flash as I bent to look through the smeary window. Shona bristled and put her hand protectively on the bonnet of the car she had been bought for her eighteenth birthday. The man was too busy looking at Shona's legs to notice this gesture of ownership.

'Great little run-around,' he muttered as his gaze rose to Shona's chest. He was pushing it, I thought to myself as Shona's knuckles whitened menacingly.

We took it for a test-drive round the trading estate, driving through the piles of horse droppings, peering over the top of the cardboard price tag the man had been reluctant to remove. Shona sat quietly, one hand massaging her temples, as we crawled up Manor Road.

'At least it's red,' she offered charitably. 'It could have been yellow or anything.' I handed a pile of twenty-pound notes into a sweaty palm. I didn't bother sniffing the notes first, and nor did he.

It took me four hours to get to work that night. At one point an old man overtook me on foot and waved at me.

'Could be the plugs.' The charge-hand opened a new batch of prawns for me to thaw. 'Or the tuning.' I spent the whole shift worrying how I was going to get home again. As it turned out it was all right, just needed a bit of a warm-up and then it settled down. There were still bits of Sellotape stuck to the windscreen.

★

On Monday morning there was a knock at the door. I hadn't been in bed long, and Shona was at work, so I decided to ignore it and go back to sleep, but there was a constant tap, tap, tap, that wasn't going away. I kept visualising a beak-shaped hand eventually coming through from outside, so I stumbled out of bed and pulled on my clothes. The room smelt slightly of prawns. When I opened the door I found Maria standing on the doorstep.

'Oh, right. Hi.' I was caught out.

'Your da said you'd got yourself a flat. Can I come in a minute?'

I felt a shit as I backed away from the door and let Maria into the hallway.

'Nice place. You've done it up all right. Your da said if I saw you to get you to go round. He's not angry with you for moving out. I felt sorry for him actually.' She was staring at one of Shona's hippy poems stuck on the wall.

'I know. I've seen him.' I tried to hold her gaze, but she was curious. I mentally charged myself with information about how many earrings she had, in case one fell out. I checked she had nothing she could leave behind. I couldn't cope with her being here. At last her attention came back to me. 'Anyway, this is goodbye really. My train leaves in half an hour.'

I was relieved. I was pleased to see her, but not here. She needn't know about Shona, Shona needn't know about her. Then everyone was happy.

We were on the floor in front of the electric heater. Maria was pulling at my tracksuit bottoms. The room was charged with electricity, bolts running from my groin to my brain and back again. This incredible urge to lick my finger and stick it in an electric socket was almost too much, the thought nearly making me cum before I was inside her. She was naked, sitting astride me with hard nipples and her hair hanging over her face. Christ, the feeling was unbelievable. It wasn't just sex, but the mutual searching for something inside the other person. I checked that she still had two earrings in.

This was wrong as she writhed and pulled herself down on me. This was wrong, but it felt like the most right thing in the world, like I'd been waiting my whole life for this moment. Afterwards we lay entwined on Shona's fluffy rug. I was shaking slightly, Maria's tongue circling the line of my lips. After half an hour I was hard again, and I went on top this time. I was aching so much I couldn't have stopped if I'd wanted to. This was love, I told myself, as I came inside her. It wasn't just sex. I didn't need to have sex with Maria to be fulfilled, it was just the icing on the cake. Maria sat up, her face flushed, her eyes like stars.

'I think I've missed my train. Do you have a timetable somewhere?'

*

188

The flat looked as if it had never been lived in when I'd finished with it. A forensics team would have had no clue that Maria had been in Shona's flat. I even threw some powder over the door handles to see if any fingerprints showed. I couldn't be too careful. Shona was a cleanliness freak and very observant. Maria caught the 2.40 to Bristol. I went with her to the station and we said goodbye awkwardly. And that was that.

CHAPTER FOURTEEN

I was lost. The map I had been sent through the post was useless. I couldn't tell SN323 from G325. It was the start of my first term at college, and it was awful. The whole place was swarming with people studying maps. One girl had rolled hers into a cigarette and was trying to light it.

'Fucking thing won't even light.' She cursed and chucked it over her shoulder. It hit me right on the forehead. At five to nine it became obvious that we were all being herded in one direction. There were lecturers surrounding us and they were carefully closing in. Suddenly two great doors opened in front of us and we had no choice but to go inside.

We were in a hall of some sorts. The doors swung shut behind us and we were caught. It was dark. We shuffled into each other. Then the lights flashed on to reveal a stage. A large man with huge hands was clapping to gain our attention.

'Welcome, ladies and gentlemen,' he trumpeted, his voice deep and tuneful, 'to college.'

Options, options, options. Do I take history, sociology and creative English? Or maths, English and law? The tick box on my green form loomed at me. In the end I ticked each alternate box and trusted to luck. We had been given a wonderful pep talk from the principal about how lucky we were to be at Frome Community College. Before the environmental health people closed it down, I added to myself, as the roof groaned and creaked.

'You are the new generation, following in the footsteps of those who have been here before. You owe it to them to do your best, to work hard and to achieve your goals.'

There was a boy selling E at a table in the corner. Maybe it wasn't going to be that bad after all.

We met in the refectory at lunchtime. R567. We had all chucked our maps out hours ago and followed our noses. We had to climb over the feet of the second year students to get in. They were sitting with outstretched legs in the doorway, smoking roll-ups and farting.

All the other people on my teacher-training course were the same age or older, no kids straight from school, thank God. The oldest was a twitchy woman in her forties, who had ten children and eight foster children. She wanted to do teaching at Bath Spa. She said she got all her children together to practise on. It occurred to me that I couldn't actually give a shit about children or teaching. Listening to these people talk, it seemed that giving a shit about children and teaching was a prerequisite. I lit a cigarette when I got outside.

'Excuse me, you can't smoke those here.' It was the girl who had tried to smoke her map. I looked over to a group of students who were all inhaling and coughing. 'Oh, roll-ups are allowed,' she clarified the situation for me, 'it's just filter cigarettes are so uncool, you'll never fit in if you continue to knock your image. Trust me, I know.'

She was about sixteen. What the bloody hell could she know?

'What makes you want to smoke those anyway?' She took the cigarette from between my fingers, 'No taste, like smoking a fucking bonfire.' Her name was Gloria, she explained, as she sorted out my image problem. The coat had to go, the shoes, the bag. I needed my lips pierced, and I needed to lose weight and muscle tone. 'I still think the heroin-chic image is relevant. I don't think it's dated.' She wrote me out a diet sheet that excluded all fats and carbohydrates, and involved drinking lots of water, and taking copious amounts of heroin. I was whacked when I got home. I bought some Rizlas and some Golden Virginia from the little shop on the corner.

The front door slammed shut.

'Hi, how was college?' Shona took off her shoes and popped them neatly into the cupboard on the landing. In the box marked WORK SHOES. She came into the lounge and flopped down on the sofa. 'What are you doing?' She eyed the pile of screwed up cigarette papers on the coffee table, and the scattering of tobacco over the table, the floor and my lap.

'How does this one look?' I held out my best effort yet. It was still a bit chubby down one end.

'All right I suppose.' She was looking confused, so I showed her my shoebox.

'Have a sort-through, see which one you think's best.'

When Shona checked her answerphone, there was a message from Da. 'Hello? Christ, it's a fucking machine. Hello, has it beeped? Cameron, can you work this thing? Tell Keith to come for his tea tomorrow and to bring his bird.'

Shona wrinkled her nose.

'Wrong number.'

★

Tomorrow was Saturday. Living with Shona, that meant a clothes-shopping trip to Bath. I stood in the doorway of Dorothy Perkins and leant against the glass shopfront. The only good thing about clothes-shopping was the amount of girls that had to squeeze past me. I lit a cigarette and tried to look cool, crossing my feet and nodding my head gently to a non-existent song. I knew this girl was looking at me as she came out of Marks & Spencer. I let my gaze slide over her, stopping at her chest and then continuing down over her body. A faint blush rose over her cheekbones. Shit, she fancied me. I went red and looked away, my gaze stopping abruptly as Shona, hands on hips, came into focus. She handed me three bags and then we went on to River Island.

'I wasn't eyeing her up. She was looking at me.' There was no answer.

We drove back to Frome in silence, past the roman baths and the open-top buses, the tour guides spinning their yarn to an invisible audience. The road was full of autumn leaves, blown down from the tall beech trees that lined the way out of town.

'What time is your dad expecting us?' Shona's voice was tight and small, not exactly fierce, but displeased.

'Any time, I think.' I kept my eyes on the road ahead. It occurred to me that I hadn't met her family yet. It was a frightening thought I kept to myself.

It was the first time I'd seen the house since I'd left. We pulled up outside and Shona surveyed the scene. It was the first time she had ever seen the house that made me what I am. I could tell she didn't like it.

'Was it a definite arrangement, or a bit vague?' She paused, her hand on the door handle, hoping for a last-minute get-out clause.

'Kind of definite, I think.' I opened my door and got out. Reluctantly Shona did the same, taking in the cracked paint-work and stained walls as she followed me up the path.

The hallway was in semi-darkness. I hadn't been sure whether to use my key or not.

'Da?' We stood tentatively in the hall.

'In the kitchen, Keith.'

We went into the kitchen, which was also in darkness.

'Thanks for coming, son.' Da fixed a smile on to his face. It stayed there when he talked. It was a strain for him clearly, us coming, and the smile.

'What happened to the lights, Da?'

'Oh, the bulb blew in the hall, and now the blasted motor's packed up on the strip-light.'

'Haven't you got a spare bulb?' I went to the cupboard over the sink.

'Don't know where your mam kept them. She always did that sort of thing.'

I found a pack of unopened bulbs. As I changed the one in the hall, Shona fiddled with the kitchen light. After a lot of flickering, it came on.

'That will last you a few days, 'til you can pop to Halfords.' Shona wiped the dust carefully from her hands and looked around. The place was a pigsty, shockingly bad, and the smell was terrible.

'That's from the washing machine. The clothes have been stuck on rinse for three days and the bugger won't empty.'

Shona found a pair of rubber gloves and prised them on with purpose.

'Come on Keith, it won't take long to sort this lot out. You sit down, Mr MacNab. Would you like a nice cup of tea?'

Da brightened, and the smile which had slipped a bit, revitalised.

'Thanks, love. Are you any good at cooking?'

We had a Chinese in the end. Da had forgotten to buy any food in. We sat round the kitchen table, none of us saying much. Da's smile had disappeared altogether and he seemed a million miles away. Cameron was completely silent, probably planning his next arson attack. Takes a lot of thought, that, to strike a match and chuck it.

Before we left, Shona fixed the washing machine. There was a shrew jammed in the outfall pipe. It must have been caught up with the washing, and been spun for a while, before it shot into the pipe like a cork.

'Bloody hell.' Da was amazed. 'That wouldn't have happened with a mouse.'

★

Shona suggested we went swimming at the weekend. I was in no position to negotiate. She drove her Fiesta which was sensible considering, while I sat in the passenger seat, gripping the PVC cover in fear. Ever since Tam had tipped over our bathtub boat when I was twelve, I'd had this obsessive fear of drowning, being trapped under the surface, the air being pushed out of my lungs by a growing tide of liquid, the feeling of hands on my neck, holding me under.

'This is meant to be fun.' Shona informed me, taking her

195

eyes off the road to survey the panic in my face. 'Exercise is good for you.'

I threw up just outside Shepton Mallet, the smell of the sewage works pushing my fragile stomach to the limit. There was a pale orange splash on the door handle. Shona opened the glove compartment and handed me a box of Wet Ones. I looked across the green hills and fields on either side of the road, and my legs ached longingly. There was exercise, and there was torture. Swimming was the latter.

'We're over half-way there. I didn't realise you got car-sick.'

I didn't. I could travel for miles with my eyes shut, facing backwards, with the smell of fried eggs in my nostrils, providing the destination wasn't a swimming pool.

The water was warm as I slipped into the shallow end, 'slipped' being the operative word, because I tripped over a CAUTION sign and fell in head-first. As I regained my footing and surfaced, chlorine stinging my eyes, Shona was patiently blowing up a pair of bright orange water wings. 'Safety first, first aid last,' she announced solemnly as she strapped them firmly on to my arms. I watched Shona swim up and down, counting the lengths with a grim look on her face. I bobbed at the side, my hand never out of reach of the edge. The armbands were making my skin sore, bright red pressure points that went white when I pressed them.

It wasn't too bad really, I thought to myself after, drinking hot chocolate in the restaurant, now the water was out of sight, and I knew the pool would be closed for six weeks for repairs. Shona was into swimming, the result of her entry into this world via a birthing pool, she reckoned. It struck me that we really didn't have an awful lot in common. Mam had me on her back with her feet in stirrups. Perhaps the way you were born shaped your life, moulded you, was the ultimate influence on who you were going to be. Maybe Mam was watching *The Towering Inferno* when she went into labour with Cameron. I'd had a difficult birth, according to Mam, long, drawn out, and I was the wrong way up. It occurred to me, as it had often done, that maybe this was my first time round as a human. It was a constant learning process which was why I cocked it up so often. I could smell chlorine on my hands as I opened the car door. It held absolutely no memory for me at all.

As a special treat we had fish and chips for supper. Well, I was allowed fish and chips while Shona purified herself with a glass of water. She watched disapprovingly as I licked the grease from my fingers.

'With your cholesterol levels, we won't be growing old together.'

I had never thought of growing old with anyone. I couldn't imagine wanting to be with her, all grey and wrinkly, with stretch-marks like Mam's and blue veins up her calves. The sex was great, it wasn't that I didn't want her, it was that I wanted other people as well. To do all there is to do, in as many different ways, with as many people as possible, and then stop. It was too early to think that's it. The thought of Shona looking like her mam, or my mam, stung the back of my eyes.

'The whole place reeks of fish.' Shona sipped at her glass of water and turned the telly on. I hated feeling this depressed. It was eating at me. I didn't know how to make it go away.

★

The next day I woke to the sound of horse's hooves. I looked at the alarm clock. It said ten to ten. Shit. I'd forgotten it was Da's hearing today. I was supposed to be there at half-nine.

There were only a few people in the court. Da was sitting in the witness box, wearing a suit that was slowly strangling him. It was the suit he had got married in, when it was acceptable to wear green Dralon. He had worn the same suit to his dad's funeral and to Mam's dad's funeral, And he had got the flares taken in and worn it to Tam's funeral. It was his lucky suit (without the luck). We listened to the evidence and saw the evidence and then the jury tried to decide whodunnit. Our doctor said his piece about extenuating circumstances while Da looked at his shoes. I bet he wished he hadn't accused old short-arse of banging Mam over the back of his consulting chair now.

The defence for the RSPCA presented the jury with their photo evidence: large colour prints of the dead sheep. I studied my nails, I didn't want to look, to go through the crash all over again. Da looked truly sorry sitting there, his top lip sunk into his bottom one, the light catching on the shine of his suit jacket.

It was all over by twelve. Shona had finished her copy of *The Stage* and was looking round for something to eat; Da was trying not to smile too broadly in case the judge thought he was being brash and doubled his punishment. We accumulated on the steps outside the court. An animal rights campaigner banged on the roof of the car as we drove away.

'Maybe things can start going back to normal.' Da breathed air deep into his lungs.

Normal. Things could never be normal, things never had

been normal. Maybe abnormality is normality. It was a comforting thought.

Shona was quiet in the Griffin that night.

'Seems a bit bloody light if you ask me. He killed all those sheep, but in six months time he can buy some more, and do it all over again.' She stared at the bottom of her glass.

'It would have killed him if he'd had a life ban.' It wasn't like me to defend Da.

'So if you get killed in a car crash, and he does it again, that's all right too is it?'

The RSPCA representatives had looked mutinous as the judge read out his verdict. A member of the public screamed out, 'You fucking murderer,' and spat at Da across the benches. A chant of 'Murderer, murderer, murderer' drifted round the room. Cameron, who was sitting next to me, smiled with relief. I watched him nervously, hoping to God that he wasn't planning to burn the whole place down afterwards. I had made a point of removing all the matches from the house when we went there for tea. I even looked down the back of the sofa, and in the warming drawer of the Aga.

In six months Da could buy himself some sheep and start again, with Cameron as front man instead of Tam.

'I'm going to give Da some money, so that he can keep the land on.' I traced the ring of beer on the table with my finger. She was a bloody good actress I had to admit. I almost believed the look of horror on Shona's face.

'You are joking, right? You only have a few hundred quid left. You're not chucking that away as well, you need that money for your car.'

'It will help keep Da going. He's worked for years on that

land, and there's nothing to say that I can't own any sheep. We could buy him a few ewes.' I was on a roll. With the minimum investment I could help Da and Cameron in one go.

'But you don't even get on with him. Keith, we need that money.'

★

Gloria was waiting outside college when I arrived. She was smoking a roll-up.

'Hiya, Keith, you're looking good.' She was wearing a small tight T-shirt with I'M TOUCHY-FEELY written over the front. I took out one of my roll-ups and lit it.

'What baccy are you smoking?' She sniffed the air, breathing in my smoke. 'That's Golden Virginia that is, that stuff's shit, that's poof's baccy. You wanna smoke some with more tar, much more flavour.'

She followed me to my class. I wanted to hit her. I wanted to shag the pants off her.

Shona was sitting on the bedroom floor with a plastic bin liner. She had emptied my drawers and was stuffing my clothes into the bag. She was so absorbed in what she was doing, she didn't notice me come in.

'What's going on?'

She jumped and looked up. What had I done? What had I done that she had found out about?

'This stuff has got to go. It's all full of holes. I can't believe you go round wearing rags half the time. And don't say you can't afford anything new, because you can afford to give your money away.'

My heart calmed itself. I wasn't wearing a T-shirt that said

200

I TOUCHED GLORIA'S TITS IN THE TOILETS AT LUNCHTIME.
'I'll get some new clothes this weekend, if you like. I need some decent stuff for college.'

After tea I cleared the plates and chucked the muck in the bin. We didn't wash it straight down the sink here, like we did at home. I could hear the cha-cha-cha-cha of the sewing machine, as Shona altered one of her costumes. In the bin I found a postcard with a picture of the Tower of London. The handwriting was Mam's.

> Tues. High drama from the start, plane hit turbulence over the Channel and we nearly came down. Posting this from the airport. Hope you are well. Missing you. See you at Christmas, Mam xxx

'What's this doing in the bin? I hadn't seen it.'

Shona looked up and smiled, not hearing a word I'd said. I waved the postcard and she took her foot off the pedal.

'I thought you'd finished with it. It's been on the worktop for days.'

I tried to imagine what it would feel like if Mam got killed, to think of her body floating in the Channel until it was picked up by rescuers, or left until it got so heavy with water it sank to the bottom of the sea. Not the best way of dying, drowning. You puff up too much.

She shouldn't have gone; Da was right. Not when she had responsibilities. I popped home for an hour and told Da and Cameron about the postcard. They'd had one too, depicting Big Ben.

There was a fight outside the flat that night. I woke to the sound of screaming and cheering as one dark figure pushed another against a car with a thump that reverberated across the street. There was music spilling out into the night, a fast beat that swung open the part of you that stores adrenalin, letting it flood out, fuelled by drink and sex. My watch said 2 a.m.

'Leave it, leave it.' A voice deep with adolescence, intervening, trying to pacify but only inflaming the figure who really didn't want to leave it. A girl, in some way connected to the brawlers was screaming, 'Bastard, bastard', fear making her stutter, but still sounding confident, with the sort of bravado you have at sixteen.

Shona was still asleep. After a day of being tidy, nothing could wake her. I got out of bed and stood quietly at the window. I could feel my heart beating. It was like watching a scene in a film, with a soundtrack overlaying the action, but it was different as well, not controlled, raw teenage angst lashing out all over the place, and I was glad to be in here and out of it. For the first time the flat started to feel like it was mine. One figure was on the ground now, clutching at himself, telling the other to fuck off in a hoarse sob. I lay back in bed next to Shona and felt relieved that I had missed out on all that.

★

The market was busy on Wednesday. The stench of sheep crap and greasy wool was overpowering. The town was plastered with posters informing us that the circus was coming, fluorescent orange rectangles that caught the corner of your eye. I tore one down and stuffed it in the bin. I was in a rare good mood, feeling for once that change could be good as well as bad. I was sussed, an octopus with its legs pointing to parts of my life. One leg led to work, another to the flat, another to Shona, the fourth to my career, the fifth to my family, the sixth to my new business interest, the seventh, to my adulthood. It was the eighth leg that I hadn't planned for.

★

There was a knock at the door early next evening. Cameron stood with his back to me, studying the landing. He had trouble looking directly at me since the night he had burnt down St Mary's. 'There's a woman been looking for you in the Griffin, and in the White Horse, says she needs to talk to you urgently.'

I looked behind me. I could hear Shona brushing her teeth in the bathroom. She always stood very still when she did that, so as not to mess the taps up.

'What woman?'

'Dunno, some right old dog.'

There was only one old dog who would want to speak to me.

'Cheers, Cameron, I'll sort it.'

'She really is an incredible hag.' Cameron looked directly at me for the first time. I could see his brain whirring.

'I've got something here for you,' It was a bad time, but it changed the subject. I fished a self-help book off the telephone table.

'I got this for you at the library.' I had looked under P for pyromania.

Cameron looked blankly at the text, and then back at me. 'Cheers Keith, but I already know all there is to know about pyromania.' He turned and started his descent,

'It's supposed to be a self-help book. Chapter Four is particularly good.' I called after him, but I don't think he heard.

CHAPTER FIFTEEN

It had been three months since I had last climbed those piss-stained stairs to her flat. In my mind I had tried to wipe her out. I had shifted the schema of things and had actually lost my virginity to Maria. It suited me better that way. Maria was my first love. Shona 2 was my second relationship. Shona 1 was the result of a row with my girlfriend and thirteen pints of beer. One of those terrible mistakes that you shut right out of your head.

The stairs still smelt of piss. Whatever else changes, at seven o'clock in the evening someone will always come and piss on the stairs here. It was comforting.

There was no answer. I knocked for fifteen minutes. I sat down on the doormat and waited. I must have fallen asleep, because I had this incredible dream that Shona 1 was standing naked in front of me. She was a DD cup and when she turned, and bent over, her arse had filled out, the razor bones hidden by soft flesh. I had a massive hard-on, and the imprint of the mat on my face, the smell of cat urine very faint on my hair. Shona looked down at me through her red eyes.

'Darren?'

I sat up. What a terrible shock. She was far, far worse than I could ever have remembered. A dog, a hag, her lips, a leaf skeleton, her skin, the colour of cheap fuel, stretching over cheekbones you could whittle arrowheads on.

'It's Keith actually,' I reminded her. 'All right?'

The flat was in a state. A blood-soaked sanitary towel lay on the kitchen floor next to the bin. There were full ashtrays everywhere, a faintly fishy smell. Shona poured me a large whisky, neat, from a near-empty bottle. It went straight to my head.

'Well, congratulations.' Shona took off her shoe and chewed her big toenail. She looked up and spat a piece of nail on to the carpet. She smiled suddenly. I tensed instinctively. 'Congratulations on becoming a daddy.'

Shona switched feet.

Looking out of the window, I could just make out Cley Hill in the distance, its off-triangular summit rising up out of the top of the Spar, framed in the foreground by pigeons pecking in the guttering and adding the occasional sliding pile of grey shit to the roof tiles. Mam always said that pigeons carried more diseases than rats, which was probably true seeing that a lot of viruses are airborne. I had a sudden urge to go to the toilet.

We had to press a buzzer before they'd let us into the ITU. I was numb and number.

'Even I know that you have to be pregnant for nine months Shona. It can only be six.' I was watching a film. A film where this pig-ugly woman tells this sorted bloke that she has had his baby. Only when I tried to turn the telly off I found the pig-ugly woman was still there.

'He's in the intensive care unit. He was born at twenty-four weeks gestation. The doctor says he has a one per cent chance of survival, but he's really strong. And don't try to pretend he's not yours. It's been a long time since anyone else has offered to fuck me.'

There was a bottle of surgical scrub on the sink, where we washed our hands. The smell reminded me of Maria after the termination. We put on white coats, like the ones the doctors wore but cheaper.

'He's in the end incubator.' The nurse smiled and pointed, 'You're little one's daddy are you?' My nose started to prickle, my blood vessels just waiting to explode. It was all too fast. I looked for the end incubator. The word 'incubator' made me think of chickens and eggs. I wasn't prepared for what I saw.

'Justin, meet your daddy.' Shona was behind me, touching my elbow. A name. It had a name, a really crap name. It was lying on its back. It could have been a string of fairy lights there were so many wires. I bolted.

I caught the bus to Cley Hill. I needed to walk and climb, to stretch the muscles that were growing flabby. When the ache started to burn up my legs, I walked faster, the pain from my calves blanking everything. From the top I could see into outer space, it was so clear. I hauled myself up on to the stone monument and could hear my heart tennis-balling across my chest. My feet hung over the head of some late flowers; I couldn't remember the name any more.

'I thought I needed a shit, kept going back to the toilet and pushing and pushing. I thought when I dumped I'd go down the hospital. I knew it wasn't right.'

It felt as if it was all over. The octopus had been caught in a net and was waiting to be eaten, his tentacles sliced off one by one. What a fucking stupid thing to happen. I was eighteen. I couldn't get Shona's face out of my head, like this kid had erased the other one. She no longer had a dead baby, just a baby. My fucking baby. Perhaps this one would die too. A one per cent chance of survival meant that there was a ninety-nine per cent chance that it wouldn't.

★

I went to work, went home, went to bed and got up again. I likened myself to a nuclear reactor. If they could shut down, so could I. It worked after Tam died. Just don't talk about it and it can't get you.

The baby had been one pound and three ounces. There had been no heartbeat when it was born.

'The surgeon rushed him off to this little room and pushed this canister of air into him.' Shona waved her cigarette, gesticulating wildly, high on adrenalin from reliving the trauma. Well, high on something. I reasoned it must have been oxygen they pumped into the baby. I buried my head in my hands, trying to hide the emotional bone I just couldn't chew right now.

'They said he was dead and then they wheeled him out. I didn't want to look. Thought they were doing some kind of therapy, like they did with Crawford.' She paused for dramatic effect, and to take a puff of Ventolin from an inhaler between drags of smoke.

'His little mouth was opening and closing like a fish. He was so small, like an Action Man. All the nurses were crying and hugging each other.'

I cooked myself bacon and eggs. I hummed along to a song on Radio One, a cover of the Smith's 'Girlfriend in a Coma'. I still had a copy of the original.

'He has this bleed in his head from where he was born. The consultant said it was only mild to moderate.' Shona stubbed her fag out under her Hush Puppy.

'I can't believe that I've had another baby. I'm over forty.'

Christ. I had no idea she was that old. I changed the sheets on the bed, hoovered the lounge and washed the kitchen floor. Then I put the bin out and went down the road for a paper.

★

The sheep arrived on the Monday in a big transporter. Ten quality Cheviots, organically reared and in prime health. Da chose the Cheviots, felt he could do with a change. Shona came to watch as the ramp was lowered and the sheep tore off up the hillside where some piles of hay were waiting.

'These ones have got thicker necks. He'll have trouble hacking their heads off.' She spoke under her breath and started picking bits of fluff from her scarf. 'Or now we're part of the EU, perhaps Cameron could set fire to them, that would be right up his street.'

In a moment of weakness I had told her about Cameron's problem.

'Why don't you go home? I won't be long.' There seemed little point in her staying.

'OK, fine. You know where to find me.'

She was pissed off, but I pretended not to notice as I signed a bit of paper the driver was holding in front of me. He leered at Shona as she picked her way out of the mud. 'She's a bit of a cracker. Nice arse.' The man was not aware of Shona's obsession with cleanliness, her habit of sterilising cutlery with a lighter in restaurants.

'Yeah, she is.' I signed my name with a squiggle.

Da closed the wooden gate.

'Hinges have dropped. I'll have a look at it tomorrow.'

'I'll give you a hand if you like.' It felt good to be out.

Shona was heavily into rehearsals. I felt I was slowly going mad stuck in the flat on my own.

'You're on. Now, how about I buy you a drink down the Griffin?' Da rubbed the cold from his hands.

'Just a quick one.' I gestured in the direction of Shona's retreating nice arse.

'Don't worry. We won't keep you long. Cameron, stop farting about and come down the pub.'

It was Christmas Day. It was early evening and everywhere was hung with a spider's web of streamers from a whole pack of party poppers. The lounge was draped in paper chains we had made at school, and there was a cardboard angel swinging limply from the light fitting. Mam was washing up endless plates in the kitchen, and Da was asleep on the sofa, having drifted off after watching the *Only Fools and Horses* Christmas special. Tam was out. He hadn't been about since first thing.

There was a lighter on the coffee table, half hidden by Monopoly cards. Cameron pulled it out and started to flick it on and off. His eyes glued to the orange flame with the lick of blue gas. There was a streamer dangling by his head and he held the flame to it. A millimetre of pink flared and crumbled. He did it again, reducing the streamer a bit at a time. I watched transfixed, my hand frozen in a chocolate selection box. With a little whoosh a green piece of streamer caught and held the flame. It burnt upwards faster than we could watch. It connected with a paper chain, which lit instantly, and soon there was a burning train chugging its way round the room, sending out tiny puffs of smoke. The chain train stopped at Angel Station. I watched, a Crunchie going soggy in my mouth. The angel's doily wings caught first with a spitting hiss, and then the toilet-roll body flared and dropped straight into Da's lap. Da woke with a start, a full whisky glass slopped into his lap. The angel liked a drop of Bell's, it had to be said. The fire really took hold, reflecting in Da's eyes as he came to grips with the burning sensation on his trousers.

'Fucking hell. Christ all-fucking-mighty.' Da leapt up and started hitting himself. Its damage done, the angel slipped to the floor and went out. I looked round for Cameron. There was a slight breeze from the open door. Da focused on me, and the lighter at my feet.

'You little cunt.' He bellowed. 'You spiteful little cunt.'

Mam spent the rest of the day picking fragments of a whisky glass out of my face.

★

Shona was in bed when I got in, pretending to be asleep. She didn't even stir when I puked the contents of my stomach on to the bedroom floor, six pint's worth. It was only when I was scraping the floor with my trousers, trying to clear the mess, that she muttered: 'Use the Vanish with some hot water and a towel,' without even moving her lips.

She was still pissed off next morning, nearly slamming my hand in the cutlery drawer when I went to get a fork. 'I'm sorry about yesterday. I got caught up.'

'You were putting some sheep in a field. How caught up can you get?' She neatly cracked the top of a boiled egg with her spoon. I winced.

'We went to the pub. Da wanted to buy us a drink.'

'I expect he did. It's not often a son gives away all his money like that, and why not spend it in the pub?' Shona left

210

her egg, grabbed a sanitary towel from a pack on the table and stormed to the toilet.

Gloria was waiting for me when I got to college.

'Hi, gorgeous,' she called out.

I was embarrassed to think of the incident in the ladies toilet a few weeks back. We had shared a joint at breaktime and she had shown me a scar on her ankle. I had shown her one on my arm. She showed me one on her thigh and I showed her one on my stomach. Then she pulled up her top, revealing a huge braless pair of tits.

'See if you can find it' she urged. I had a good look, and a feel and no, she'd got me, I couldn't find one at all. Then she remembered it wasn't on her chest but her foot. The bell went at that point; I went to sociology, and she went to law.

'Are you avoiding me?'

'No.' I was. I fancied her like mad. She turned me on something chronic, but I couldn't cope with the complications. I didn't need this right now.

I bought a new CD in Woolworths and a bag of assorted toffees. Shona would be home from work now. She would be wondering where I was. I stood on the bridge and threw wrappers at the ducks, who pecked at them with their beaks. It was Friday evening. The clocks had gone back a week ago, the final wave bye-bye from summer, the promise of a disgusting wet six months ahead. The town was full of the sound of accelerating cars, the signal of another end of a working week, the start of a long weekend. I was missing Maria, needed someone to lament with me on how I had fucked up my life. All around me blinds were being pulled down, hiding the glass-fronted shops underneath, and I wished that eyes could close like that and blot everything out, problems locked out with a padlock till morning, because when my head hit the pillow my mind sped up, jumping from frame to frame, two and two only ever making five. I walked back through the silver town, shielding my face from the glare of a low sun on metal.

Cameron popped round to see me that night. It was only the second time he had been there. I noticed he was wearing a pair of trainers like mine. Shona wasn't impressed to see Cameron and made a show of putting all the matches and lighters in a locked tamper-proof box, which she then hid in the bedroom.

'You want a drink mate?' I had rarely been in a one-to-one situation with Cameron. Shona left to go to her rehearsal and we sat down next to each other.

'Yeah, a tin would be nice.'

When I brought a six-pack in from the fridge he was flicking through the self-help book.

'Still got it then?'

'Yeah, it's overdue at the library. I can't afford the fine.'

Cameron picked at a thread in the suite Shona's mum had given her as a flat-warming present. 'It fucking gets to me sometimes.' Cameron looked up, focusing slightly to the left of me. Or I focused slightly to the right of him. 'It's all mapped out for us. All we can ever achieve is to be as wasted and fucked up as them.' I presumed he was talking about Mam and Da. I took a swig of my drink and tried to think of something poignant to say.

'Don't be daft. It's not like that,' I lied, snapping the end of my ring-pull and floating it inside the can.

We sat in silence for ten minutes while I tried to figure out why I hadn't agreed with him. It was odd, knowing that he felt the same as me, though he wasn't capable of changing anything like I was. It struck me that he was the ultimate victim of our family, whereas up till now I had always thought it was me.

'Da's well stoked about the ewes.' Cameron finished his drink and looked round, not sure whether he should drop the empty can on the floor like he did at home.

'Good.'

'Is that your jacket in the hallway? It's cool.'

He really didn't have any personality of his own, I thought to myself when he left later. He was an incubus, sucking the personality of other people. I scrawled down Gloria's phone number for him to take away.

'Cheers, I'll give her a ring. Shona's a bit of a cracker as well. If you ever get bored with her.'

'Yeah, yeah, you'll be first in there.'

He looked quite cheerful when he left, whereas I had never felt so miserable in the whole of my life.

★

Shona was having a pre-winter clean. I made myself scarce, though I had nowhere to go. Before, I would have popped in to see Maria. We would have gone for a walk or sat and chatted in the garden, as I showed off my knowledge of plants and wild flowers. I was dislocated. Floating in orbit, not able to land and not able to spiral off into space. The logical thing would be to try to land, without crashing.

I stopped at the park. but the swings were busy so I sat on the roundabout with one foot on the ground and half ran, half sat as we picked up speed. I stopped at one point to pick up a couple of passengers. Both were the same age as me, both looking as miserable as fuck. One had a scar of baby food healing on his shoulder; the other was completely anonymous. We all sat in silence and went round and round for over half an hour, our feet trailing the ground. It was reassuring, that other people were just as miserable as me, and I thought that misery was a sign of maturity, that the kids you saw out on a Friday night, laughing and shouting, had all that to come. 'Grab your happiness where you find it,' was a motto that could be handed down, because when it's gone, it's fucking gone, and then you spend the rest of your life acquiring new layers of misery, until finally you die of some miserable disease.

Shona would be hard at work on the net curtains, washing them in bleach or some other fucking crap that she bought from Sainsbury's. A year ago all I had to worry about was how clear the sky was, now I didn't care enough to even look. Tam was gone, Mam was gone, Maria was gone. I made a decision as I walked back along the tarmac path and through the little gate.

Da was cooking a roast when I knocked at the back door. 'Hello son, just in time. Grab yourself a seat.'

'Is there enough?' Shona never cooked a roast because she couldn't abide greasy plates.

'We'd welcome the company.'

I sat down as Da served up beef with potatoes, carrots and peas. I cut up my meat with a fork. The carrots were cold and the peas like bullets, but the meat was perfect, rich and crumbly. Da poured gravy over his vegetables. Cameron looked up.

'Pass the salt, Keith.'

★

There were religious nutters swarming around Trinity, ringing bells and shouting the odds. I watched them as I threw my clothes into a Spar bag. Shona was sitting in the lounge, her hands cupped round her face, an open copy of *Take a Break* forgotten on the table, along with a half-drawn template of a device to catch toenail clippings. It was terrible.

'Why, why, what the fuck went wrong?'

I looked at my hands, 'I don't know.'

'Is there someone else?'

I made myself look at her, feeling like complete shit. I pulled out a Polaroid picture from my pocket.

'No.'

She looked from the photo to me without comprehension. The baby was lying on a white sheet, its hands pulled into fists up to its chest. One huge head on a bag of bones.

'You bastard, you fucking bastard, you bastard.' Shona sat down on the sofa and started pushing her fist down her throat to stop herself crying, but she made herself gag instead.

'And to think I thought you were a virgin, you were that crap.' She screwed the toenail template up and threw it at me, along with the copy of *Take a Break* and some sample clippings. The nail scissors caught my back as I left the room. I left the key in the key box in the hall, on the hook labelled KEITH'S KEYS, HOME. The door clicked shut behind me as I started on the flight of stairs, with my two carrier bags.

*

215

I sat on the step outside for an hour with my bags. I had never felt so dislocated in all my life, never felt so much a part of nothing. An old lady walked past. She was staring at me, cross for messing up the pavement; she probably thought I was a tramp, or sky-high on drugs.

'Spare some pennies for a shot of heroin missus.' I put out my hand. Before I knew what was coming she had whacked her walking stick into the palm of my open hand. It fucking hurt like mad. I sucked wildly at my hand, trying to take away the sting. A huge welt was swelling rapidly. When I looked up I saw the back of the bitch's dress as she disappeared into Help the Aged. I fought the mist in my eyes as I gathered my bags and walked home.

My bedroom was how I left it: shit-brown with holes in the paper. The walls were comfortably close together, four straight with no complications. There was still the mark where the telescope had rested on the windowsill, still the remnants of the spider's web round the window. I thought of Auntie Fran and the six grand that she left to me, Tam and Cameron. And how we had spent it. I lay down on the bed with my boots on and wiped mud over the pile of sheets I had put out. It was good to be home.

Five minutes later my bags were back in the hallway.

'Sorry, Keith. I didn't think you'd want to move back in. I let the room last week.'

CHAPTER SIXTEEN

The black bag was moving slowly, watched by next door's cat, which had learnt to lift the latch on the shed window. It was council policy that bin bags should only be put out on bin days and not before, so as not to detract from the unspoilt beauty of the town; a town that was slowly falling down, propped up by council rejuvenation schemes. So the rubbish was kept in the shed. It was hot for October; I was still wearing shorts. I opened the wooden door and watched the bag with interest. It was moving at quite a pace, heading towards me, and beyond to freedom. Some silly mouse or vole I thought to myself as I fished in my pocket for my pen-knife and slashed the plastic bag down the middle. Next thing I remember is the back of my head hitting the floor. I got up, and before I went down again I saw a writhing mass of maggots, in tins, on a chicken carcass. The contents of the bag were nearly indistinguishable. And the bag was still moving. I hit the floor.

★

Winter hit like a flannel on the back of your neck. One day it was sunny, the next raining. The chimney sweep's van could be seen all over town. The gypsies moved on again. The fields turned to mud, then to syrup. It was so fucking depressing, sleeping on the lounge floor during the day, and then working through the night. For the first time I managed to save some money, though. I thought about Maria a lot, lying on my duvet as Cameron and Da watched the sport. I hadn't heard from her. An enormous ache was building up inside.

I popped into town for a takeaway. I walked up to Badcox and banged at the Indian but the door was locked and the blinds down. The Singh's had sold up a few months ago and moved to London. This new lot obviously hadn't quite got the hang of the business yet. When I got back Gloria was sitting in the kitchen, drinking tea. She was wearing a top so short I could see her stomach, which was such a beautiful shape it was difficult to tear my eyes away. I hadn't seen her for a while, because I was missing a lot of my classes. The realisation that I hated children made me think teaching wouldn't be a vocation for me. Anyway, my evening was certainly looking up. She looked dead shaggable.

'Hiya, Gloria, all right?' I didn't know she even knew where I lived, though I did vaguely remember her writing her address on the back of a chewing-gum wrapper.

'Hi, Keith. Cameron and I are going to see a film in a minute.'

I could be so, so stupid sometimes. The surge of blood that was rapidly shooting downwards took a change of direction, hitting my cheeks full-on. Not much chance of a shag there, then. 'Oh, right.'

Cameron grinned at me. He had translucent teeth; I'd never noticed that before. I felt a small jolt inside as his gaze met me bang-on.

After they left, Da's lodger came in, a refugee who had been placed here by the council. All his family were dead. Everyone he had ever known was dead.

'Hello, hello, hello!' He was all smiles.

'Good news?' I asked him.

'It's just a beautiful day in a beautiful country.' He hummed as he put out the ironing board and filled the steam iron. Personally I would think he'd get on Da's nerves, which were frayed at the best of times. His arthritis, which had calmed down during the summer, was playing him up, and his whole leg from the hip down was twisted. It was best to stay out of his way in the mornings. He hadn't really changed that much at all, and as before I seemed to be the trigger that emptied the barrel into the air. The powder monkey, stuffing the cannon with gunpowder with the inevitable explosion one lit match away.

Mam phoned as Romani was putting the board away again.

'Keith?' The line was terrible, crackling and breaking up. 'Why aren't you at Shona's?'

'I can't hear you, Mam.'

'How's everyone?'

'Fine. What's it like out there?'

The line went dead before she could reply.

'Oh that's usual.' Romani smiled cheerfully. 'It means the cable's been hit. Your mam's been there a few weeks, hasn't she? It's good she hasn't been killed yet.'

Hadn't anyone told him the war was over?

The agency phoned to say there was no more work at Smarts. Prawn cocktails were off the menu this time of year, it seemed. A few weeks working there was seriously jeopardising my relationship with seafood: I tended to buy jumbo sausages from the chippy, I noticed, rather than cod. Anyway, I couldn't spend the rest of my life shovelling prawns. I needed to find a decent job before the Child Support Agency caught up with me, if the kid was still alive.

I climbed the piss-stained stairs for what turned out to be the last time. When I got to the flat the door was open and some old bloke I didn't know was stuffing Shona's things into black bags. 'If you're after the flat, see the council, laddie.' The man tied a knot in the bag he was filling and stood up. He was huge, well over six foot. He sounded Scottish. It occurred to me that this old boy was Shona's dad.

'Where is she?' The place stank. I looked into the hall. It was dark. The curtains in the lounge were closed.

'Is it money you're after, because there isnae any.'

'I'm a mate.' I had to say something. I couldn't say that I called on Shona for sex when I needed it and she wasn't able to say no because she was so fucked up.

'She's dead. Died sitting in the chair with a bottle of whisky and the phone on her lap, only it had been disconnected so she couldn't ring anyone.' The memory of Auntie Fran flashed past. I leant against the doorframe.

'Dead?' I thought of Cameron then, telling Mam.

'Alcohol poisoning. Some shite got her pregnant and then pissed off as soon as the wain was born. I don't give a double fuck what his reasons were. He killed my daughter.'

Alcohol poisoning, I thought as I let myself out. From the stench of the place you'd think it was ammonia poisoning. I wasn't upset that she had died in particular, it was just that everybody kept dying. It was unsettling.

★

I thought I ought to go to the funeral, which was held at St Mary's portakabin on the Friday. We waited over an hour for the coffin to arrive, standing by the borrowed lychgate and staring at concrete slabs. Opposite a crane was knocking down the old factory units that had once been the old printing works, The site was full of bobbing yellow heads, like daffodils on a roadside.

'You should have brought her on time,' Shona's dad hissed at the undertakers as they pulled up. 'My daughter was such a punctual person.' He looked to me to reinforce this, but I looked away. I didn't really know her that well.

It was pissing down, so we huddled inside. It was a squash, what with the coffin. I stared at the cheap wooden box. It was weird, being that close to someone dead. The vicar said a lot of nice things about Shona, though there were only two of us present, and we both knew that he had only met her once, at the hospital after Justin was born, when she had asked to borrow a fiver for a taxi home. I wondered if he had ever got it back. Shona's dad kept putting the vicar off his stroke by saying 'Aye' after every biblical quote. It was the same vicar who had buried Tam. As we all walked back out into the rain, Shona's da shook my hand and thanked me for coming. I was wearing Da's suit, the lucky one.

'It's the wain I feel sorry for. He'll never know who his parents were.' He wiped a piece of mud off the shiny leg of his trousers.

'What will happen to him?'

'I'm a sixty-five-year-old widower. I live in a tenement in Lesmahagow. I cannae look after myself, let alone the wee fellow. I'll put him up for adoption.'

'Right.' I put out my hand and it was grasped with real affection. 'Bye then.'

'Bye, Keith, thanks for coming. It's a relief to me that at least one of her friends was decent.'

I walked off, feeling incapable of feeling anything real ever again.

★

Shona and I sat on the edge of the lake at Shearwater, our legs resting on the steel netting that kept the stones in place. There was a wooden sign behind us warning fisherman not to use peas or beans as bait. It had got impossible, that ache. I was missing Maria so much I had picked up the phone and dialled Shona's number. Shona was unwrapping a birthday cake. She placed it on her lap, stuck five candles in it and lit them.

'I'm sorry I forgot it was today, Shona.'

Shona looked up at me, hurt magnified in her eyes. It was going to take a lot of grovelling before I could get rid of the ache. The lake was busy, full of little yachts with fluorescent sails. I prised a stone from under its cage and lobbed it into the water.

'How's fatherhood?' Shona watched me with bright eyes. I could tell there was an emotional drama just around the corner.

'I never meant to hurt you. I'm so sorry. These past few weeks I've been doing a lot of thinking. We could get married, if you want?'

'A wife *and* a baby. Shame we're not related, how bloody cosy that would be.' She bit into the cake. Well, it was worth a try.

'No thanks.' Shona licked her fingers. 'I'm seeing someone else anyway.'

*

Cameron had his tongue down Gloria's throat when I got in. The taps were on in the kitchen, the water nearly running over the sink.

'Why are the taps on?' No answer.

I sat at the kitchen table and read the local paper. Some residents were up in arms because structural faults had been found in the foundations to their houses, which had been built in the 70's. The area involved ran adjacent to where Auntie Fran had lived. HOUSE SHOCK ROCKS NEIGHBOURHOOD the front page blared out at me. Lucky Fran's house hadn't been affected, or our inheritance would have amounted to nothing. After her funeral I remember Mam storming in with a bag of bin liners from Poundstretcher's, sorting through drawers and cupboards. In a shoebox under the bed she had found three human toes, belonging to Fran's husband, who had died of a stroke a few years previously.

'That's love for you.' Mam put the lid back on the box. I was sitting on the floor, making a tower out of some old teacups; Tam was sorting through the garage, looking for tools for the car that he was too young to buy. Mam went quiet for a bit, staring out of the window. I didn't understand what she meant, so I stared out of the window as well. The toes had dropped off one by one, the blood supply not reaching George's foot, apparently. I sneaked a look in the shoebox when Mam went downstairs to start on the lounge. They were greenish in colour, the skin flaking off into the cotton wool they were resting on. I picked one up. It was hard, like a twig. I sniffed it then put it back and replaced the lid. Maybe Mam was right after all: a box of toes said far more than sex.

The sheep were sheltering behind the barn as I took Da a flask of tea. It hurt him too much to walk back to the house at midday. Tam had erected the barn; he had worked for days, carrying huge tin panels up on his shoulder and banging them into place, like a giant Meccano kit. Da was peeling a banana, sitting in the corner on a bale of mouldy hay. One of the sheep sniffed at the banana skin on the floor. Da aimed a kick at its head and then his face buckled with pain.

'Wrong bloody leg,' he gasped. I left him there, crouched, rubbing his leg, eating his banana, and climbed down the hill and into the kitchen.

The new road was well under way now, I noticed. The trees had gone from the valley floor and there were mounds of building materials everywhere, like giant molehills, or ingredients on a TV cookery show. Two men were erecting a new sign: a yellow background with a huge M. A rusty JCB with smashed windows had been daubed with red paint. The name 'Whattell' on the original white sign had been scribbled into 'Fuckall', in protest at something that couldn't be stopped. The big boulder I had pushed over the top of the hill was now completely covered in moss. Da had gone mad about the boulder, blaming its removal on some local kids. That is why he now sat on a bale of hay.

The kitchen was flooded, three inches of water slopping round the floor. The tap was on in the sink, and the sound of orgasmic screams was coming from the lounge. A hundred years worth of dirt had washed from the stone floor. Underneath I could see blue quarry tiles, big slabs practically impossible to shift. I splashed my way to the sink and turned the taps off. The plug was in.

'Cameron, what the fuck have you been doing?'

Cameron appeared from the lounge, wearing a pair of boxer shorts. His face was flushed. 'Shit. I forgot I left that on.'

I left him and Gloria cleaning up the mess and went over to the pub. When I came home Da was sitting at the table reading a paper and I could hear music coming from upstairs. When I opened the swing top of the bin to throw some rubbish in I found a can of petrol and several boxes of matches.

'I've decided to retire.' Da made me jump. He was still looking at the paper.

'Oh, right,' I replied, and then mentally kicked myself. I really must stop saying that.

'I asked Cameron to take the sheep on, but he doesn't want to.'

'Oh.'

'You can run them if you want. If not, I'll get shot of them.' He was throwing them back in my face. Da looked at me, quite genially. 'It's too much for me, on my own. Cameron has got himself a job in town.'

Mrs Brownlow called at the house at teatime. I was in the middle of stuffing my face with a large piece of fruitcake when Da led her into the kitchen.

'That won't make you grow. Won't give you any muscles.' Her cistern was blocked. She wanted me to go and fix it. I knew nothing about cisterns.

'Can't the plumber do it?' I flushed the cake crumbs down my throat with tea.

Da frowned. 'Plumbers cost the earth. It doesn't cost anything just to have a look, Keith.'

The house smelt of budgies as we went inside. By the look of the aviary, it could do with a muck-out again; the corpses were beginning to foul up the lowest perch.

'Toilet's up there.' Mrs Brownlow pointed up the stairs.

'Right.' The stairs were carpeted in frayed brown, which was coming away in places. I peered down the pan, which was cracked and stained and devoid of water. 'It's empty.'

Mrs Brownlow was already on her way downstairs. I pulled the chain a few times, but it was jammed completely. I bent forward and thought about the film that was due to start in twenty minutes. Downstairs the front door opened and I could hear Mrs Brownlow talking to her neighbour.

'Are you going into town later, dear? Can you pick me up some Trill from Pet's Pantry?'

There was a splitting crack on the back of my head that made me fall forward. I banged my chin on the toilet bowl, which smelt of piss. I could feel absolutely nothing, but knew something terrible was happening. There was something next to me on the floor, something cold and hard. I tried to shout to Mrs Brownlow to say something was wrong, but I wasn't sure what and the words didn't come out anyway. I could smell blood, and I realised it was coming from me. Shit, I thought, I'm fucking bleeding. There was a pause after this revelation for what seemed like hours, but it must have been a split second. I stood up unsteadily, and there was a mirror in front of me, but it wasn't me I saw, it was a face completely soaked in blood, a red face, like a devil, or an England fan emblazoned with the Union Jack, only it was only red. I knew I had to get out. I turned, and there was something in the way, hard against my calves, but I was superhuman and could push past it. I was Spiderman, with my red mask, and I half flew, half fell down the stairs and on to the mat. The front door was closed, Mrs Brownlow's voice getting more distant. I shook my head, tried to get my eyes to focus. The door was spotted with red and an overwhelming panic hit me, an incredible shot of adrenaline that slapped round my body, enabling me to open the latch and I was out of that door and into the street, and cars were hooting and people screaming and I lay down by the double yellow line and waited for a traffic warden.

★

I woke to bright lights and the feeling that my brain was being squeezed. I opened my eyes and touched my head. I was wrapped up in the sheet somehow. An awful ache was thumping above my eyes, which were on strike, my pupils marching round with little banners saying MORE RIGHTS FOR RETINAS.

'Wakey, wakey.' A voice sounded by my left ear. I tried to turn but I couldn't.

'Maria?'

'Try again.' The voice sounded again, drier this time.

'Shona?' My eyes focused on the freshly scrubbed face. It suddenly occurred to me that I was in hospital.

'Where am I?' It was a stupid thing to say, seeing I'd just worked it out.

'In hospital.'

'Why am I?' That was a better question.

'A cistern came off a wall and stove your head in.'

My hand instinctively reached for my head. The sheet, I realised, was in fact a bandage. 'You were doing an old lady a favour. You're practically a hero.'

It was a film I'd seen once, about a dog that rescued a kitten from a fire. Everybody patted the dog and wanted to give it a home, but next morning it was gone, couldn't settle. I knew how it felt. I wasn't sure if there was a trace of irony in Shona's voice. 'What are you doing here?'

Shona sighed and got up, brushing imaginary creases from

her skirt. She looked right here somehow, with the bright lights and shiny floors.

'You get some rest.' She bent forward to kiss my cheek. A strong smell of Listerine and Persil made me jump. 'I expect your nerves are shot to pieces.'

Da came to see me later. He took my hand. It was a move I didn't feel comfortable with but I didn't like to take it away. His hand felt dry and callused. Years of Mam nagging him with a bottle of Neutrogena hadn't softened him at all.

'That's the second of my sons I've seen on that road.' Da wasn't talking to anyone in particular. 'What have I done to deserve that? What am I being punished for?'

I was booked in for a scan that afternoon. The cistern had fractured my skull in two places, the doctor said, and he wanted to monitor the bleeding.

'I'd cancel your Mensa membership for this year,' he joked. 'It will take a while before your picnic basket is full of sandwiches again.' All the nurses laughed, and the technicians. Da didn't. Nor did I.

★

Shona took the key out of the ignition and turned to face me. We were in the carwash in Duke Street. A few lines of raggedy bunting straggled across the road. Shona put her fingers on the back of my head and felt around. It was two weeks since they had discharged me from hospital.

'You could stick a tennis ball in there,' Shona commented. I needed to know this like I needed a hole in the head.

'Is this thing going to come on then? I don't think you're quite up to the barrier.'

Shona withdrew her hand. 'Don't worry, I expect your hair

will grow over the gap. It's lucky the bit that's thinning is near the front.'

My hand shot to my head in horror.

'Oh, don't worry, it's not obvious to everyone. It's just when you look closely.'

The tormented anguish of my reply was drowned out by the sound of heavy water. Visibility vanished amid the torrent of water that was being sprayed at the car. In front of us, through the haze, we could see green heading towards us. Shona's hand slipped to my trousers. 'God, there's something really sexy about water.'

I leant forward for her tongue, which I sucked greedily. It had been so long. Shona sighed and sat astride me. All I could hear was the drumming on the roof of the car and the slow whoosh of the rollers as they went over. This raw need was building inside me as I wiped myself against her and pushed inside. We were moving fast, in rhythm with the jet of water. It was too fast, causing my knee to scrunch against the armrest, so we slowed to the movement of the roller, gently smoothing over the bonnet, the roof, the boot. I could feel myself coming as the wax-bar headed towards us. I thought it was going to smash through the windscreen and decapitate us, but at the last minute it soared up and over and I felt Shona sigh and relax on to me.

'I do want to marry you, if you still want to, I mean.' Shona spoke into my shoulder. I pulled myself out and wriggled for some air.

'Course I do,' I lied.

All the way home Shona talked with bright eyes about our future together. The ache was still there inside me, and I didn't know why. I finally realised that it was over between us, and that I didn't want to see her again.

'August is a lovely month for a wedding.' Shona squeezed my leg.

I got Shona to drop me off near the market and made my way across town to the hospital. I knew it quite well, what with Maria's termination, the baby and my head. I found the paediatric ward and looked through the glass window of the special care unit. There was a baby in an incubator there. I didn't know if it was my baby; it was just a baby, a very small one, with strands of hair and a million tubes. I turned and walked out again. It was weird. Two weeks in hospital, with my kid in the next ward, and no one knew. I sat on the swings in the park and wondered where the fuck I'd gone wrong.

★

We went to Weston-Super-Mare, me, Da and Cameron. Cameron drove the Granada and I sat in the back, in an area that kept increasing. It was the wrong time of year for Weston, I thought, as Da bought a ticket for the car from a fluorescent warden. We walked along the front in silence, the words whipped from our lips by the wind. The kiosks were closed but we managed to buy an ice-cream from a van on the corner. We sat in the shelter with the tramps, eating our 99 cones. I shivered into my jumper. The tide was out about twenty miles, the golden sand of my childhood, winter grey.

'Used to be donkeys when you kids were little.' Da shifted the weight from his bad hip. They were probably off skiing this time of year. We walked along the shore, leaving a trail of footprints, all virtually the same size. We were going at Da's pace, painfully slowly, one long stride then a shuffle. My legs felt under-used; they needed stretching, the muscles reawakening. I could have run along the shore, racing the seagulls

230

and the tide, a finishing post marked by a distant sandcastle, but I walked sedately, slightly in front of the others.

'It's just the three of us now,' Da said without any affection. Cameron was looking at a boat out at sea, with a half-smile on his face. Thinking about Gloria, I told myself. He wasn't really with us at all. Da had hit the nail on the head. It was just the three of us, and that's what I didn't want. I wanted it to be just me. This was about me now, not Tam or Maria, or Shona or Shona, or the baby. The ache which had been building up inside me was starting to fade, was settling into a throbbing hum that I could learn to live with. The past, I repeated to myself, is that. Keith MacNab begins here.

★

We were at the top of Cley Hill, me, Tam and Cameron. It was early spring. The grass hadn't begun to grow, and a few snowdrops straggled across the flat summit. The wind was whipping our hair into straight lines that changed direction as we ran round and round in circles. Da and Mam were rowing in the car, the remnants of my birthday tea littering the back seat. Two birthday cakes were in Tupperware boxes on the floor. There always had to be two cakes: Cameron used to cry unless he had one as well.

I climbed on to Tam's shoulders and heaved myself on to the stone monument. I looked out over the valleys.

'Years ago this was the look-out to a whole civilisation,' Tam steadied my feet. 'Around you, can see everything needed for survival. Water from the stream down there, nuts from the wood, grazing for the livestock, and this, even a place to bury the dead.'

The power of what Tam was saying hit me. I could feel the adrenalin pumping through my body. I stood up on the narrow stone and felt the wind tugging at me, but I was invincible.

'I'm the king of the castle.' The words whipped away from me. Suddenly I felt Tam's grip on my feet slacken and as I looked down he grinned at me, then gave me a little push.

I fell. First I fell ten foot to the grass under the stone, then I rolled and, unable to stop, went crashing over the ledge and straight down the steep slope. Faster and faster I rolled, down and down, the grass burning my bare skin, bracken scratching my arms and legs. Mam and Da both jumped and looked up as I crashed down on to the bonnet of the Granada. In the distance I could hear the words: 'No you're not.'